Beowulf

Grendel

John Gardner

Curriculum Unit

Mary M. Lindenberg

The Center for Learning

Beowulf/Grendel is Mary M. Lindenberg's first Center for Learning curriculum unit. A teacher of British literature, Ms. Lindenberg follows a successful approach to old English poetry by presenting the modern *Grendel* as a clarifying counterpoint to the characters and theme of *Beowulf*.

The Publishing Team

Rose Schaffer, M.A., President/Chief Executive Officer
Bernadette Vetter, M.A., Vice President
Amy Richards, M.A., Editor

Cover Art

Clare Parfitt

List of credits found on Acknowledgments
page beginning on 77.

ISBN 1-56077-139-9

Contents

Introduction

Because it is the only full-length epic extant from the Anglo-Saxon period of English literary history, *Beowulf* is an important work for students of English literature to study, and it is usually the first work which students meet in an anthology-type text. However, its antiquity, ceremonial poetical style, and boastful hero may be inaccessible to modern students. Teachers may wonder how to make such an ancient hero palatable. In fact, the poem is as full of suspense, scenes of action, and blood and gore as any afficianado of today's horror movies could wish. Its monsters and dragons are as fiendish and frightful as any "Freddy," its young hero as daring and hopeful as any young man or woman who wants to make a mark on the world; its fight scenes are as full of action and suspense as any "Speilberg" could concoct with all of his Hollywood equipment. But the only technology necessary for the appreciation of *Beowulf* is the mind's eye translating the vivid words of an ancient singer into pictures for the imagination to view.

The nature of heroism, the virtues of Anglo-Saxon kingship, the loyalty of kinsmen and sworn followers are some of the themes explored in this work. The Viking fascination with the sea, a fascination which continues in the consciousness of the English island nation, is one thread woven throughout the poem. Forming the warp and woof of the story is the Beowulf poet's interweaving of Christian belief in one God with the old Scandinavian pagan acceptance of fate on which his ancestors relied before embracing Christianity.

To the Anglo-Saxon, fame was all-important because it alone transcended the limitations of time and the inevitability of death. The struggle for fame was the pathway of the hero, and his renown was spread by the scop, the Anglo-Saxon poet, who sang of his glorious deeds. Beowulf exemplifies the ideal Anglo-Saxon hero and king.

Though the poem is long and full of ceremonial language, its lack of end rhyme is similar to the free verse of modern poetry. Its marked rhythm should appeal to teens who respond to the strong beat of modern music. Since the best scops composed as they sang, telling the story using alliteration, rhythm, and interchangeable stock phrases, students should recognize that Anglo-Saxon poetry and rap music have several elements in common. In addition, kennings, clever metaphorical phrases or compound words, appeal to students' appreciation of riddles. Vivid detail brings the story to life and supplies much information about the lives and ideals of early ancestors. The challenge of monsters and their defeat by a young hero who relies on God and his own strength symbolize for students their own fears and future struggles. For young readers, the advice of the old Danish king to the young Beowulf and the aging Beowulf's final battle with the dragon provide important insights about leadership.

John Gardner's *Grendel* is a modern novel told from the point of view of the first monster whom Beowulf kills. It is short, ending with Grendel's death. For students, its chief value lies in the light it throws on some aspects of the story in *Beowulf*, the use of the first person point of view, and the demonstration that an ancient story can inspire and interest a interest a contemporary reader. *Beowulf* does not reveal Grendel's motives for feuding with the Danish King and killing his men; *Grendel* examines in detail the development of the monster mind of Grendel. Gardner also gives the reader an interesting explanation for questions about Unferth, a character who is somewhat of a puzzle in *Beowulf*. Into the main narrative in *Beowulf*, allusions to other Scandinavian legends are woven whose relevance is not always easily seen. Gardner's recounting makes their relevance obvious.

Reading *Grendel* along with *Beowulf* provides an excellent opportunity to teach how an author can influence a reader's sympathies and judgments by the viewpoint of the narrator of the story. The monster, Grendel, who enthralled an ancient audience is no less fascinating to a modern reader.

Teacher Notes

Beowulf is significant for its place in literary history as well as its eminence as heroic poetry. The lessons in this unit stress the story and the poetry. Once students know the story, they need to understand how the poetry functions in keeping the thread of the narrative.

The poem may be read aloud by students or teacher, or a recording may be used.

In choosing a translation to use other than in an adopted anthology, the following may be helpful: both Burton Raffel's and Charles W. Kennedy's translations are available in paperback. Raffel's language is more contemporary and his book less expensive than Kennedy's. These lessons are based on Kennedy's translation. Because teachers using these lessons may be using a different translation, only limited page or line numbers are given.

Grendel is primarily valuable for the amplification and insights it provides for the story and characters in *Beowulf*. It contains vulgar language and the tone is dark and pessimistic. The lessons emphasize the novel in relation to the poem *Beowulf* and seek to help students see that the real theme is that Grendel is wrong: the world is not meaningless.

John Gardner

1933-1982

John Camplin Gardner, Jr., was born on a farm in Batavia, New York, on July 21, 1933. After graduating with a B.A. from Washington University, St. Louis, in 1955, he went on to receive a Ph.D. from the State University of Iowa in 1958. His subsequent teaching career in medieval literature and creative writing took him to colleges and universities throughout the country, his last position being at the State University of New York at Binghamton.

Gardner wrote fiction for fifteen years before succeeding in publishing his first novel, *The Resurrection*, in 1966, but the years that followed saw a prolific output of fiction. His third novel, *Grendel*, appeared in 1971, and *October Light* (1976) won him the National Book Critics Circle Award for fiction. His final novel, *Mickelsson's Ghosts*, was published in 1982. As well as novels, he also produced short stories, collected in *The King's Indian* (1974) and *The Art of Living* (1981). An epic poem, *Jason and Medeia*, appeared in 1973, and a radio play, *The Temptation Game*, in 1980. Gardner wrote several books for children and three opera libretti, and his *Poems* were published in 1978.

Although best-known for his creative writing, Gardner was also a respected scholar, writing several works on medieval literature and publishing a modern English version of *The Complete Works of the Gawain-Poet* in 1965. A polemical theoretical book, *On Moral Fiction* (1978), made him a controversial spokesman for the moral responsibility of literature. He was also the founder and editor of the magazine *MSS*.

Gardner was married twice and had two children from his first marriage. Four days before a planned third marriage he died in a motorcycle accident on September 14, 1982, near his home in Susquehanna, Pennsylvania. [1]

[1] Harold Bloom, ed., "John Gardner" in *Twentieth Century American Literature*, III: 1546-1565 (New York: Chelsea House Publishers, 1986), 1546-1547.

Lesson 1
Beowulf—Background and Setting

Objectives
- To identify the setting and time of the poem
- To become familiar with the characters

Notes to the Teacher

Beowulf is an English poem, yet the setting is northern Europe in what is now Denmark and Sweden. The events described probably took place at the same time as the invasions of England by Scandinavian tribes from Denmark in the fifth and sixth centuries. After the first foothold in c.440, the Angles, Saxons, and Jutes inhabited most of England by the middle of the sixth century. Although Beowulf appears to be a fictional character, Hygelac, Beowulf's uncle and king, is an historical character who was killed in battle c.521. The story includes Beowulf's early adventures in Denmark through his succession to Hygelac's throne after the death of both Hygelac and the son whom Beowulf helped to succeed him. Thus Beowulf's story occurs in the homelands at about the same time the first Englishmen were migrating to England and establishing themselves as a dominant culture.

Beowulf consists of two parts: first the story of Beowulf's defeat of the monster, Grendel, and his hag of a mother, to save the Danes, a tribe in what is now Denmark; second the fatal battle in which Beowulf defeats a dragon in defense of his own people, the Geats, a tribe in Southern Sweden. No one knows who first wrote the story of Beowulf, but scholars believe it was first composed in its present form during the eighth century. One of the flowerings of Anglo-Saxon culture occurred during the eighth century, and most of the poetry which has survived was written during this time. It is likely that the poet who wrote *Beowulf* used existing heroic lays of the oral Anglo-Saxon tradition brought to England by his ancestors from their Scandinavian homelands. It seems evident that the poet meant to work in and pay tribute to this heroic tradition when he composed *Beowulf*. The earliest copy is a tenth century transcription made by two scribes which is now in the British Museum.

Procedure

1. Distribute **Handouts 1** and **2** before beginning the reading of the poem. Ask students to mark **Handout 2** according to the directions and information on **Handout 1**. Have available a map showing Northern Europe and England. Suggested Responses: *see map and timeline on page 2.*
   7. *Denmark and Sweden*
   8. *1265 years*

2. As students read the poem, direct them to trace the routes which Beowulf travels during his adventures.

3. Distribute **Handout 3**. Assign groups to research and present oral reports on the topics listed.

4. Distribute **Handout 4**. Explain that this handout will help keep the various characters and tribal groups clear.

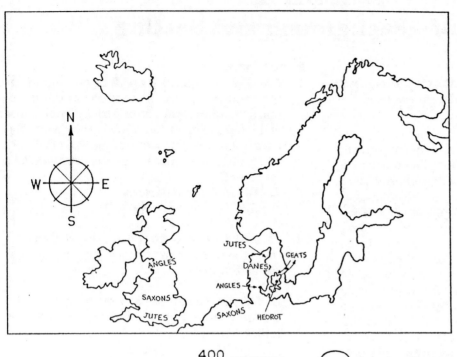

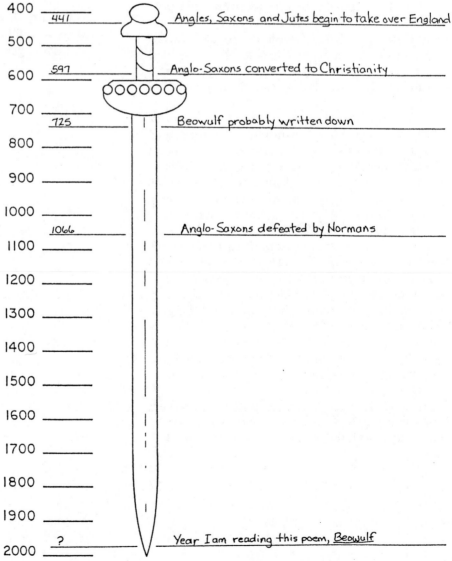

400	
441	Angles, Saxons and Jutes begin to take over England
500	
597	Anglo-Saxons converted to Christianity
600	
700	
725	Beowulf probably written down
800	
900	
1000	
1066	Anglo-Saxons defeated by Normans
1100	
1200	
1300	
1400	
1500	
1600	
1700	
1800	
1900	
?	Year I am reading this poem, _Beowulf_
2000	

2

Name_____
Date_____

Back to the Ancients

Directions:

1. *Beowulf* is a poem about a hero named Beowulf who belongs to a tribe called the Geats who lived in what is now Southern Sweden. On your map (**Handout 2**), write the name *Geats* in the area of Southern Sweden.

2. In the story, Beowulf goes to the aid of a group of Danes who lived on the island of Zealand, part of what is now Denmark. Place a dot on the map and label it *Heorot*. Write the name *Danes* in the area of Denmark.

3. On the map mark the names of the three tribes, Angles, Saxons, and Jutes, who came from Scandinavia beginning in 441 and ousted the Celts, eventually dominating England. Place them in Denmark: Jutes in the north; Angles in the South, and the Saxons near the coast just south of Denmark. They are the first Englishmen, and they controlled England for 600 years until they were defeated by the Normans in 1066.

4. On the map of England, write the names of the three tribes: place the Angles in the north; the Saxons in the south; and the Jutes along the Southern coast. On the timeline (**Handout 2**), mark and identify the year 441 and the year 1066.

5. When the Angles, Saxons, and Jutes came to England, they didn't know how to write, but they had a rich oral literary tradition. They learned to write when they were converted to Christianity beginning in 597. Mark and identify the year 597 on the timeline.

6. The Anglo-Saxon culture reached a peak during the eighth century. Most of the poetry that survives dates from that time. *Beowulf* is thought to have been written about 725. Mark and identify this date on your timeline.

7. The Anglo-Saxon writer of *Beowulf* is considered to be a scholar and a Christian. He knew his own history and culture, the Scriptures, and it is likely that he knew Latin literature as well. It is probable that he used the oral sagas and legends of his ancestors as the basic material for his epic. It is important to realize that although *Beowulf* is the only full-length English epic that survives from the Anglo-Saxon period, its setting is not England but _____ and _____ .

8. *Beowulf* is an ancient poem. On the timeline mark and identify the year in which you are reading this poem. How may years have passed since that Old English poet began to write his heroic epic? Can his eighth century words possibly stir the hearts, minds and spirits of twentieth-century readers? On your own paper write a paragraph or two describing your feelings as you prepare for this assignment. Be honest. Use the following as your opening.

> About _____ years have passed since an unknown Anglo-Saxon wrote down the story of the Geat hero, Beowulf. As I anticipate reading this ancient poem, I feel . . .

Name_____
Date_____

Where and When

Directions: Use the map and the timeline to follow the directions on **Handout 1**.

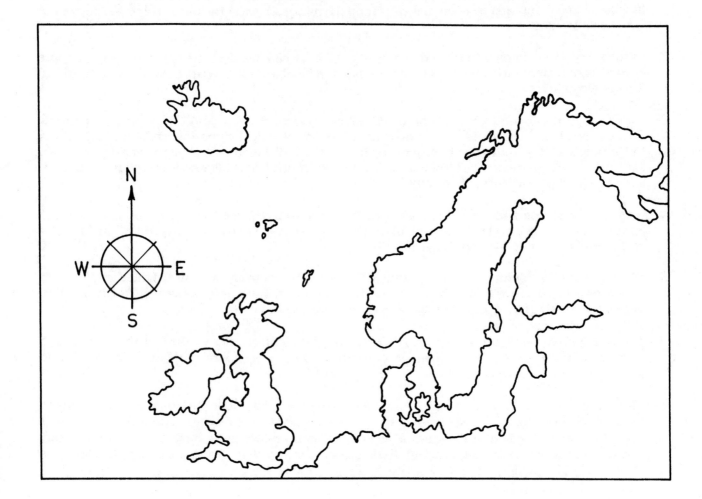

Name_____
Date_____

The Sword of Time

400 _____
500 _____
600 _____
700 _____
800 _____
900 _____
1000 _____
1100 _____
1200 _____
1300 _____
1400 _____
1500 _____
1600 _____
1700 _____
1800 _____
1900 _____
2000 _____

Name_____

Date_____

Feuding, Fighting, and Praying

Directions: Research and present an oral report on one of the following Anglo-Saxon topics.

1. Government: Aethelbert; Alfred, the Great; Edward, the Confessor; Harold; Offa; *bretwalda; witan;* Danelaw

2. Warriors and weapons: thane; feud; wergild; sword; scramasax; spear; shield; helmet; armor

3. Sutton Hoo

4. Society: *Earl; coerl; gebur; cotsetla;* hide; status of women

5. Entertainment: scop, gleeman, mead, mead-hall

6. Religion: pagan Gods: Woden, Tiw, Thunor, Frig; Wyrd; Christianity; Augustine; Paulinus; King Edwin

7. Art and Culture: illuminated manuscripts; *Lindisfarne Gospels; Anglo-Saxon Chronicle;* Venerable Bede; *History of the English Church and People;* Caedmon; Cynewulf; runes; Golden Age of Northumbria

8. History: Hengist and Horsa 441, 449; Celts; Romans; Angles, Saxons, Jutes; Vikings; Danes; William, the Conqueror; Battle of Hastings; Norman Conquest

9. Monsters: *drauqr; ketta;* trolls; giants and elves of Norse myth; goblins; ogres; dragons

Sources:

Abrams, M. H., Ed. *The Norton Anthology of English Literature.* New York: W. W. Norton & Company, 1979.

Blair, Peter Hunter. *An Introduction to Anglo-Saxon England.* 2nd ed. Cambridge, England: Cambridge University Press, 1977.

Brooke, Stopford A. *The History of Early English Literature.* Freeport, New York: Books for Libraries Press, 1982.

Crossley-Holland, Kevin. *Green Blades Rising: The Anglo-Saxons.* New York: The Seabury Press, 1975.

Clemoes, P., Ed. *Anglo-Saxon England,* Vols. I and II. Cambridge: Cambridge University Press, 1963.

Davidson, H. Ellis. *Gods and Myths of Northern Europe.* Harmondsworth: Penguin, 1964.

Donovan, Frank R. and Kendrick, T. D. *Vikings.* New York: Harper, 1964.

Grohskopf, Bernice. *From Age to Age: Life and Literature in Anglo-Saxon England.* New York: Atheneum, 1968.

_____. *The Treasure of Sutton Hoo.* New York: Atheneum, 1973.

Leeds, E. T. *Early Anglo-Saxon Art and Archaeology.* Clarendon, Oxford and London: Oxford University Press, 1968. New York, 1968.

McHargue, Georgess. *The Impossible People.* New York: Dell Publishing Co., Inc., 1972.

Quenell, Marjorie and C. H. B. *Everyday Life in Anglo-Saxon, Viking and Norman Times.* London: Carousel, 1972.

Sellman, R. R. *The Anglo-Saxons.* London: Methuen, 1959. New York: Roy.

Name_____
Date_____

Genealogies of the Royal Families

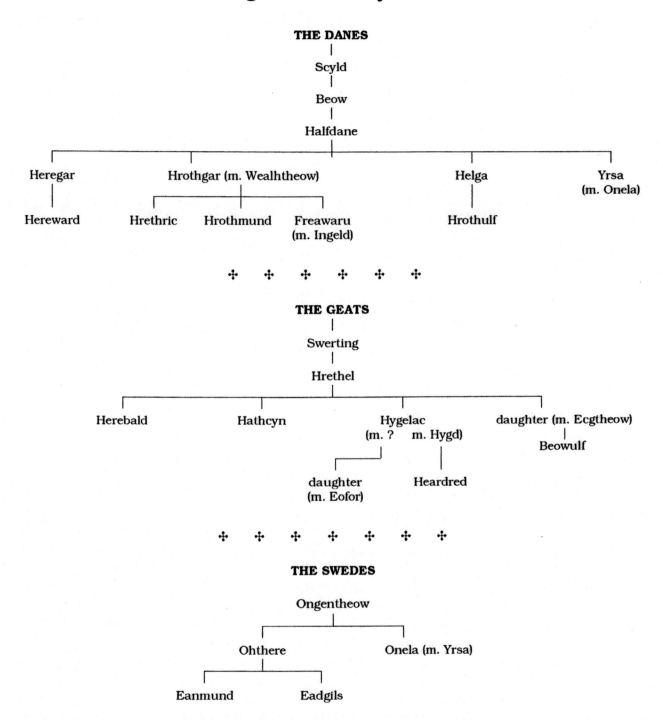

THE DANES

Scyld

Beow

Halfdane

Heregar   Hrothgar (m. Wealhtheow)   Helga   Yrsa (m. Onela)

Hereward   Hrethric   Hrothmund   Freawaru (m. Ingeld)   Hrothulf

✣ ✣ ✣ ✣ ✣ ✣

THE GEATS

Swerting

Hrethel

Herebald   Hathcyn   Hygelac (m. ?   m. Hygd)   daughter (m. Ecgtheow)

Beowulf

daughter (m. Eofor)   Heardred

✣ ✣ ✣ ✣ ✣ ✣ ✣

THE SWEDES

Ongentheow

Ohthere   Onela (m. Yrsa)

Eanmund   Eadgils

Fig. 1.2. Ruth P. M. Lehmann, *Beowulf* (Austin, Texas: University of Texas Press, 1988), 119.

Lesson 2
Language and Style

Objectives
- To recognize and scan the rhythm of Anglo-Saxon poetry
- To identify and explain kennings
- To have students understand that they are reading a translation of *Beowulf* and to recognize some of the difficulties involved in translating a work of literature

Notes to the Teacher

Beowulf was written in the tradition of alliterative verse, the style of poetry which the ancestors of the *Beowulf*-poet brought to England from their homelands in Scandinavia. The heroic poems were sung by trained singers, called scops, who sometimes composed them extemporaneously for the entertainment of the king and his warriors at celebrations in the mead-hall. The scops were much honored by the Anglo-Saxon kings and people because they were the keepers of the history and mythology of their countrymen since the Anglo-Saxons, until they became Christians, did not know how to write or read. A good scop spread the fame of his king by composing songs about the exploits in battle of the king and his warriors and comparing him to the ancient heroes of saga and song. Many warriors would flock to the mead-hall of a famous king to share in his glory.

The language used by the *Beowulf*-poet is Old English, which is so different from modern English that we would need to learn it like a foreign language before we could understand the original poem. Therefore, the modern student usually reads a translation. The translation used for these lessons is by Charles W. Kennedy in *Beowulf, The Oldest English Epic*, published by Oxford University Press, copyright, 1940 and renewed in 1968. This book is available both in hardbound and paperback editions.

There are, however, many different translations, even prose translations. Each translator determines how faithful to the original, in style and meaning, his translation will be. The translator must be a poet as well as an expert in Old English and a scholar in ancient English and Germanic literature. He must also contend with the fact that the oldest copy of the poem has been damaged by time and by fire and is not the original, but the work of two scribes who probably made errors in their copying.

Some textbooks condense the poem leaving out lines and passages, especially those that allude to stories of other heroes and battles not directly related to Beowulf's adventures.

The characteristic style of Anglo-Saxon poetry consists of a line with four stressed syllables, a pause or *caesura* dividing the line into two half-lines, and no end-rhyme. The stressed syllables are alliterated, and there is no set number of unstressed syllables. The poet also uses a metaphor called a *kenning*. Kennings are descriptive comparisons, such as "whale-road" or "sail-road" for the sea, "bone chamber" for the body, or "candle of heaven" for the sun.

Procedure

1. Distribute **Handout 5**. Read orally or listen to a recording of the first 37 lines of *Beowulf*. Ask students to work in pairs to complete the handout. Discuss their responses.
   Suggested Responses, Part A:

   Lo! we have listened//to many a lay

   Of the Spear-Danes' fame,//their splendor of old,

   Their mighty princes,//and martial deeds!

   Many a mead-hall//Scyld, son of Sceaf,

   Snatched from the forces//of savage foes.

   From a friendless foundling,//feeble and wretched,

   He grew to a terror//as time brought change.

   He throve under heaven//in power and pride

   Till alien peoples//beyond the ocean

   Paid toll and tribute.//A good king he!

   Suggested Responses, Part B:
   1. *No rhyme*
   2. *Alliteration: the l's in Lo, listened, lay. Answers will vary. Examples can be found in nearly every line.*
   3. *Alliteration serves as a sound device like rhyme in other poetry. It emphasizes the*

9

rhythm and important words and acts as a memory aid for the scop. (Explain that in Anglo-Saxon poetry both vowels and consonants would alliterate; only alliteration of stressed syllables counted.)

4. *The number of unstressed syllables in each line varies.*

5. *There are four stressed syllables in each line. The pause in the middle of the line creates two half-lines with two strong beats to each half-line. There is no end rhyme. Alliteration is used on stressed syllables.*

2. Distribute **Handout 6** after reading the whole poem. Explain and give examples of a *kenning*. Ask students to explain the comparisons implicit in the kennings on **Handout 6**. If using a different translation, students may add kennings to the list, or make up some of their own.

Suggested Responses:

1. "Beowulf spoke; his byrny glittered,
   His *war-net* woven by cunning of smith;"
   Beowulf's chain mail armor is compared to a net used for war. Nets have openings like chain mail which prevent movement in or out.

2. "They lay on the *sea-bench* slain with the sword"
   The seashore is compared to a bench for the sea. Benches are placed around or on the edge of for sitting or resting.

3. "The *hell-thane* shrieking in sore defeat"
   Grendel is compared to a follower of hell. He is of the "seed of cain" and a follower of the devil.

4. ". . . Most like to steel
   Were the hardened nails, the heathen's *hand-spurs*,"
   Grendel's claws are compared to spurs for his hand. Spurs are worn on the heel; their points rake a horse's sides like claws scratch skin.

5. "The *heather-stepper*, the horned stag"
   The deer is compared to a creature that steps over heather, a plant which grows on the moors in England. Deer are good leapers.

6. "But the bold one had found that the *battle-flasher*
   Would bite no longer,"
   The sword is compared to something that flashes in battle. The blade of a sword catches light as it is swung in fights.

7. "As the *candle of heaven* shines clear from the sky"
   The sun is compared to a candle giving light from the sky, heaven.

8. "The *foamy necked plunger* plowed through the billows,
   The ring stemmed ship through the breaking seas,"
   The ship is compared to a horse cantering or galloping. Plunging is like the up and down motion of the horse. The prow of the ship is like the horse's neck covered with sweat.

9. Answers will vary.

3. Distribute **Handout 7**. Examine the example of *Beowulf* in Old English. Note how different it is from Modern English. Old English had letters for the sound *th*, no longer used. Word endings (inflections), not word order determines meaning in an Old English sentence. Read each of the translations aloud. Discuss the following questions.

1. At first glance, which of the example translations seems to most closely approximate the Old English? Why?
   Lehmann's translation, #3. It looks like Old English; lines are the same length, and half lines are clear.
   When the Anglo-Saxon words such as "sweord" (sword), "giganta geweorc" (work of giants), and "candel" (candle) are compared with Lehmann's translation, they appear in the same line.

2. Are all three translations faithful to the rhythm and alliteration of Anglo-Saxon poetry?
   Raffel's translation, #2, frequently ignores the pause in the middle of the line. All three have approximately four strong beats to the line. Each of the translators uses some alliteration, Raffel least of all. None use rhyme.

3. Kennedy's translation, #1, has two kennings: "Bone-rings" for vertebra and "candle of heaven" for the sun. Explain that he has translated the Old English "banhringas braec" as "broke through the bone-rings" and "rodores candel" as "the candle of heaven." How do the other two translators handle these two kennings?
   Raffel avoids the first kenning, translating the phrase as "broke bones and all" while Lehmann translates it as "bonejoints." She keeps it a compound word, but loses its sense as a kenning.

All three poets keep the second kenning with a slight difference in word order.

4. Call student's attention to diction (word choice). Kennedy calls the ancient sword a "war-brand." Lehmann describes it as a "seige-proved falchion." Raffel simply calls it "a heavy sword." Ask students to discover in a dictionary that both "brand" and "falchion" mean "sword"; both are labeled as *poetic*; "brand" also has the label *archaic*. Ask what effect the use of a poetic and archaic language has on the reader? Which do they prefer, the poetic or the simpler style? Why?

   Answers will vary. They may say that it is fitting to use archaic words to describe an ancient sword and to translate an ancient poem; poetic words make the poem sound ceremonial and underscore the heroic theme. They may prefer the poetic style because of its beauty and lofty grace or may find the simpler diction more comfortable because of its familiarity to the contemporary reader.

5. Compare Kennedy's and Raffel's translations of the incident describing what happens to Hrunting, Unferth's sword. What is the difference in meaning?

   Kennedy says that Beowulf returned the sword to Unferth; Raffel says the opposite, that Unferth gives the sword to Beowulf.

6. Ask students what they have learned about the challenges facing the translator from their examination of these differing translations. Ask if they have changed their attitudes toward the work that translators do?

   The translator must keep in mind not only the meaning, but also the style of the original and the readers of the translation. The translator must be expert in both languages and be a good writer. Attitude responses will vary. Some may be more aware of the talent and knowledge required to do veracious translating.

Name_____

Date_____

Gettin' Down with the Anglo Rappers

Directions: Work with a partner to complete this handout.

Part A: In the following lines scan (mark) the stressed syllables. Find four strong beats in each line. Draw a slanted mark (/) over the syllable which is stressed. In the middle of the line, between the second and the third strong beats, find a natural pause, known as a *caesura*. Mark its position with paired up and down lines (//). Unstressed syllables are shown with a mark like an arc on the bottom of a circle, such as ∪. Mark the unstressed syllables. This is the rhythm of Anglo-Saxon poetry. It may help if you read the lines aloud.

> "Lo! we have listened to many a lay
>
> Of the Spear-Danes' fame, their splendor of old,
>
> Their mighty princes, and martial deeds!
>
> Many a mead-hall Scyld, son of Sceaf,
>
> Snatched from the forces of savage foes.
>
> From a friendless foundling, feeble and wretched,
>
> He grew to a terror as time brought change.
>
> He throve under heaven in power and pride
>
> Till alien peoples beyond the ocean
>
> Paid toll and tribute. A good king he!"[1]

Part B: Answer the following questions:

1. Is there any rhyme, either end rhyme or internal?

2. Did you notice that often the stressed syllables in a line begin with the same letter, a poetic device called *alliteration*. In line 1, what three stressed syllables are alliterated? Find at least one other example.

3. What function does the alliteration seem to have?

4. In the lines above is there any particular number of unstressed syllables per line or does the number seem to vary?

5. Describe the meter of Anglo-Saxon poetry.

[1]*Beowulf, The Oldest English Epic*, Charles W. Kennedy, trans. (New York, London, Toronto: Oxford University Press, 1940), 3.

Wily Words

Directions: The Anglo-Saxons apparently enjoyed word-play. Beowulf is described as "unlocking his word-hoard;" a lyric describes a message as containing "wily words;" and the poets who kept alive the stories and traditions enjoyed a high status in Anglo-Saxon society. While most of Anglo-Saxon poetry is serious or even elegaic, there are ninety-five verse riddles in the Exeter Book displaying the Anglo-Saxon interest in cleverness with words. In *Beowulf*, as in other Anglo-Saxon poetry, a type of riddling metaphor called a "kenning" is used.

Find the lines containing kennings. (They are listed in order of appearance.) Explain what the kenning describes and why it is an apt comparison. On the blank lines create your own kennings or add kennings from a different translation.

1. "Beowulf spoke; his byrny glittered,
   His *war-net* woven by cunning of smith;" (p. 15)

   _____

   _____

2. "They lay on the *sea-bench* slain with the sword" (p. 20)

   _____

   _____

3. "The *hell-thane* shrieking in sore defeat" (p. 27)

   _____

   _____

4. ". . . Most like to steel
   Were the hardened nails, the heathen's *hand-spurs*," (p. 33)

   _____

   _____

5. "The *heather-stepper*, the horned stag" (p. 44)

   _____

   _____

6. "But the bold one had found that the *battle-flasher*
   Would bite no longer," (p. 49)

   _____

   _____

7. "As the *candle of heaven* shines clear from the sky" (p. 51)

   _____

   _____

Beowulf/Grendel
Lesson 2
Handout 6 (page 2)

Name_____
Date_____

8. "The *foamy necked plunger* plowed through the billows,
The ring stemmed ship through the breaking seas." (p. 62) [2]

_____

_____

9. Add your own kennings.

_____

_____

_____

_____

_____

_____

_____

_____

_____

[2] *Beowulf, The Oldest English Epic*, Charles W. Kennedy, trans., (New York, London, Toronto: Oxford University Press, 1940), 15-62, *passim*.

Name_____
Date_____

Unlocking the Word-Hoard

Directions: This Old English passage from *Beowulf* describes how Beowulf kills Grendel's mother with the ancient sword. Examine it closely. Are you able to guess any of the words? Can you point out the characteristics of style of Anglo-Saxon poetry which you have learned?

XXIII   Geseah ðā on searwum   siege-ēadig bil,
eald sweord eotenisc   ecgum þȳhtig,
wigena weorð-mynd;   þæt [*wæs*] wǣpna cyst,
1560   būton hit wæs māre   ðonne ǣnig mon ōðer
tō beadu-lāce   aetberan meahte,
gōd ond geatolīc,   gīganta geweorc.
Hē gefēng þā fetel-hilt,   freca Scyldinga,
hrēoh ond heoro-grim,   hring-mǣl gebrægd
1565   aldres orwēna,   yrringa *slōh*
þæt hire wið halse   heard grāpode
bān-hringas bræc;   bil eal ðurhwōd
fǣgne flǣsc-homan;   hēo on flet gecrong,
sweord wæs swātig,   secg weorce gefeh.
1570   Līxte se lēoma,   lēoht inne stōd,
efne swā of hefene   hādre scīneð
rodores candel.

[3] *Beowulf,* Howell D. Chickering, Jr., trans. (New York: Anchor Books, 1977), 138-140.

Directions: The following are three translations of the same passage. Compare each carefully to determine how faithful each translator has been to the original.

#1 Charles W. Kennedy, 1940

Swift the hero sprang to his feet;
Saw mid the war-gear a stately sword,
An ancient war-brand of biting edge,
Choicest of weapons worthy and strong,
The work of giants, a warrior's joy,
So heavy no hand but his own could hold it
Bear to battle or wield in war.
Then the Schylding warrior, savage and grim,
Seized the ring-hilt and swung the sword,
Struck with fury, despairing of life,
Thrust at the throat, broke through the bone-rings;
The stout blade stabbed through her fated flesh.
She sank in death; the sword was bloody;
The hero joyed in the work of his hand.
The gleaming radiance shimmered and shone
As the candle of heaven shines clear from the sky. [4]

#2 Burton Raffel, 1963

Then he saw, hanging on the wall, a heavy
Sword, hammered by giants, strong
And blessed with their magic, the best of all weapons
But so massive that no ordinary man could lift
Its carved and decorated length. He drew it
From its scabbard, broke the chain on its hilt,
And then, savage, now angry
And desperate, lifted it high over his head
And struck with all the strength he had left,
Caught her in the neck and cut it through,
Broke bones and all. Her body fell
To the floor, lifeless, the sword was wet
With her blood, and Beowulf rejoiced at the sight.
The brilliant light shone, suddenly,
As though burning in that hall, and as bright as Heaven's
Own candle, lit in the sky. [5]

#3 Ruth P. M. Lehmann, 1988

Then he saw a sword,   a seige-proved falcion
of ancient ettins   with edges tempered,
a guardsman's glory.   Though a greater sword
than any other   could ably bear,
it was the best of blades   for battleplay
featly fashioned,   forged by giants.
The champion of Schldyings   drew the chain-held sword
furiously and fiercely,   freeing it for action.
Of life despairing,   he launched a blow
catching her neck   with a cruel stroke,
so the bonejoints broke,   the blade passed quite through
the fore-doomed body,   and she fell dying;
the blade was bloody;   the brave one rejoiced.
Then a beam brightened,   burning inside,
even as above the earth   brilliantly shines
heaven's candle. [6]

[4] *Beowulf, The Oldest English Epic*, Charles W. Kennedy, trans. (New York, London, Toronto: Oxford University Press, 1940), p. 50-51.
[5] *Beowulf*, Burton Raffel, trans., (New York: NAL Penguin Inc., 1963), p. 72.
[6] *Beowulf*, Ruth P. M. Lehmann, trans., (Austin: University of Texas Press, 1988), p. 54.

Name_____
Date_____

Directions: Compare these two versions of the incident describing what happens to Hrunting, Unferth's sword.

"The hero [Beowulf] tendered the good sword Hrunting
To the son of Ecglaf [Unferth], bidding him bear
The lovely blade; gave thanks for the loan,"[7]
Charles W. Kennedy

"Then Unferth came, with Hrunting, his famous
Sword, and offered it to Beowulf, asked him
To accept a precious gift."[8]
Burton Raffel

[7] *Beowulf, The Oldest English Epic*, Charles W. Kennedy, trans., 59.
[8] *Beowulf*, Burton Raffel, trans., 79.

Lesson 3
Understanding the Story

Objectives
- To understand and to visualize the story's action
- To recognize that the Anglo-Saxons enjoyed the same kinds of gut-wrenching horror entertainment that today's Americans enjoy

Notes to the Teacher
Beowulf's fights against the monsters and his final battle with the dragon are full of vividly described action which students may not fully capture without guidance because of the unfamiliar poetic language.

The fights in which Beowulf engages Grendel, Grendel's mother, and the dragon contain the ingredients for fast-paced action scenes with suspense, surprise, movement, excitement, sword-play, fire, gore, and horror.

This lesson is designed to be limited to the planning of the scene assigned or expanded into a full-scale production including script writing, costumes, scenery, taping, and editing if time and equipment allow.

Procedure
1. This lesson should be assigned after the class has read the first third of the poem, to the point where Beowulf has displayed Grendel's dripping claw on the walls of Heorot and the Danes are preparing the celebration in the mead-hall for the victorious Beowulf and his men.

2. Distribute **Handout 8**. Read aloud while students visualize the action.

3. Distribute **Handouts 9** and **10**. Assign small groups of 3 or 4. Choose one student to act as director. Other students will be actors or prop people.

4. On **Handout 9** ask student to list the characters, such as Beowulf, Hondscio (the Geat eaten by Grendel), Grendel, the fourteen Geats, the Danes (optional); props, such as mead-benches, mead-bowls, the door, the Geat's armor, Grendel's arm. List body language and facial expressions under director's notes: Grendel's fiery eyes as he bursts in the door; the surprised, horrified expression on Hondscio's face; Beowulf's open eyes and cunning expression as he waits for Grendel to reach him; the frustrated body movements of the Geats as they realize that they cannot penetrate Grendel's spell, etc.

5. On **Handout 9** ask the director to indicate the beginning positions of the characters and their movements on the blocking chart. Use letters or symbols for actors and arrows for movement.

6. On **Handout 10**, ask students to write in camera and sound directions.
   Suggested Responses: *Students should be encouraged to use their imaginations fully.*

   Shot 1   *Camera pans over sleeping Geats in mead-hall lingering a little on Hondscio and longer on Beowulf. (Silence except for sleeping sounds)*

   Shot 2   *Cut to long shot of moors. Grendel is seen in distance.*

   Shot 3   *Quick cuts between interior of mead-hall and Grendel approaching across moors. Last cut is close shot of Grendel's face.*

   Shot 4   *Medium shot of door from inside as Grendel bursts it open. (Sounds of wood cracking and splitting and a heavy object crashing.)*

   Shot 5   *Close shot of Grendel's eyes. (Heavy breathing.)*

   Shot 6   *Dolly back and pan sleeping Geats and Grendel walking around looking at them and picking up Hondscio.*

   Shot 7   *Close shot of Hondscio's face. (His mouth opens in a scream but nothing comes out.)*

   Shot 8   *Dolly back to medium shot of Grendel licking fingers and looking for more.*

   Shot 9   *Pan sleeping Geats. Dolly in for close shot of Beowulf watching and listening.*

   Shot 10 *Medium shot of Grendel reaching for Beowulf and Beowulf grabbing his hand.*

Shot 11 *Close shot of surprise on Grendel's face.*

Shot 12 *Medium shot of struggle. (thuds, clangs, crashes)*

Shot 13 *Pan over Geats and broken mead-benches.*

Shot 14 *Dolly in to close shot of Beowulf's and Grendel's faces.*

Shot 15 *Medium shot of Geats trying to attack Grendel.*

Shot 16 *Cut to outside of mead-hall and pan over Danes listening to fight.*

Shot 17 *Cut to close-up of Grendel's face and dolly back to show him wrenching free of Beowulf and running out of mead-hall.*

Shot 18 *Long shot of Beowulf holding up arm in middle of mead-hall.*

Fade Out.

7. Optional: You may wish to let students perform and videotape the scene.

From Wily Words to Wild Action

Directions: Visualize the scene in your mind as it is being read aloud. Picture the mead-hall and the placement, movements, and body language of the characters.

"Then through the shades of enshrouding night
The fiend came stealing; the archers slept

✛   ✛   ✛

Though one [Beowulf] was watching—

✛   ✛   ✛

From the stretching moors, from the misty hollows,
Grendel came creeping, accursed of God,

✛   ✛   ✛

Storming the building he burst the portal
Though fastened of iron, with fiendish fury
And rushed in rage o'er the shining floor
A baleful glare from his eyes was gleaming
Most like to a flame. He found in the hall
Many a warrior sealed in slumber,

✛   ✛   ✛

The hardy kinsman of Hygelac waited
To see how the monster would make his attack.
The demon delayed not, but quickly clutched
A sleeping thane in his swift assault,
Tore him in pieces, bit through the bones,
Gulped the blood and gobbled the flesh,
Greedily gorged on the lifeless corpse,
The hands and the feet. Then the fiend stepped nearer,
Sprang on the Sea-Geat lying outstretched,
Clasping him close with his monstrous claw.
But Beowulf grappled and gripped him hard,
Struggled up on his elbow;

✛   ✛   ✛

He [Beowulf] sprang to his feet, clutched Grendel fast,
Though fingers were cracking, the fiend pulling free.
The earl pressed after; the monster was minded
To win his freedom and flee to the fens,

✛   ✛   ✛

There was din in Heorot
The walls resounded, the fight was fierce,
Savage the strife as the warriors struggled.

✛   ✛   ✛

That many a mead-bench gleaming with gold
Sprang from its sill as the warriors strove.

+ + +

Continuous tumult filled the hall;
A terror fell on the Danish folk
As they heard through the wall the horrible wailing,
The groans of Grendel,
Howling his hideous hymn of pain,

+ + +

He was fast in the grip of the man [Beowulf]

+ + +

Many an earl of Beowulf brandished
His ancient iron to guard his lord,
They had no knowledge, those daring thanes,
When they drew their weapons to hack and hew,
To thrust to the heart, that the sharpest sword,

+ + +

Could work no harm to the hideous foe.
On every sword he [Grendel] had laid a spell,

+ + +

Then he [Grendel] . . .
Soon found that his strength was feeble and failing
In the crushing hold of Hygelac's thane.
Each loathed the other while life should last!
There Grendel suffered a grievous hurt,
A wound in the shoulder, gaping and wide;
Sinews snapped and bone-joints broke,
And Beowulf gained the glory of battle.
Grendel, fated, fled to the fens,

+ + +

His days at an end.

+ + +

. . . the heart of the hero
Joyed in the deed his daring had done.
Laid down the shoulder and dripping claw
Grendel's arm—in the gabled hall!"[1]

---

[1] *Beowulf, The Oldest English Epic*, Charles W. Kennedy, trans., 24-28.

Name_____
Date_____

Lights, Camera, Action!

Scene

Characters in scene:

_____
_____
_____
_____

Properties List:

_____
_____
_____
_____
_____
_____
_____

Director's notes on scene:

[2] Mary Enda Costello, Paulette S. Goll, Stephen L. Jacobs, Eileen K. Maloney, *Shakespearean Comedies*, (Rocky River, Ohio: The Center for Learning, 1984), 233.

Name_____
Date_____

Blocking Chart

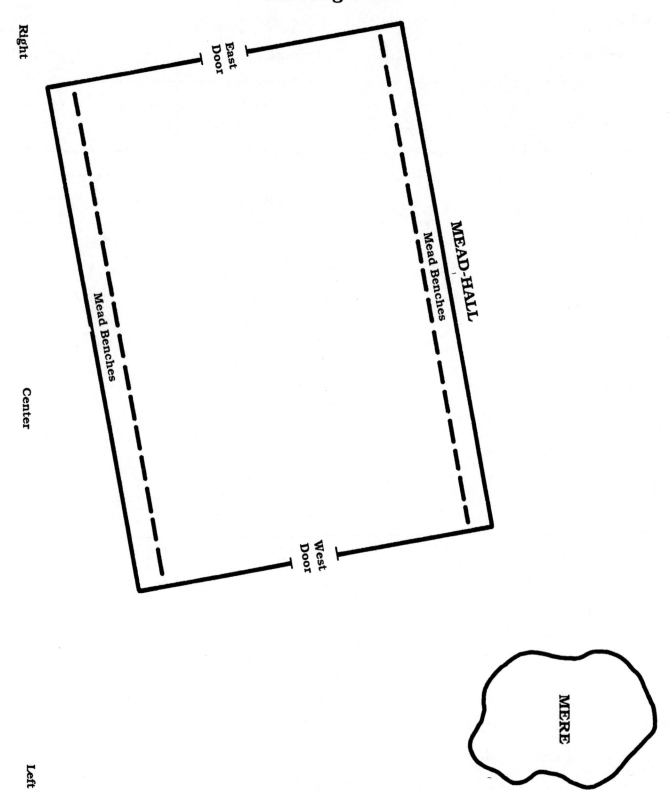

[3] Janet Goodridge, *Creative Drama and Improvised Movement for Children* (Boston: Plays, Inc., 1971, 131.

Roll 'Em

Directions: Pretending that you have one camera, write the directions for the grip (stagehand). You may want to use the following camera terms:

fade in—opening screen goes from dark to light

fade out—opposite of fade in; used between scenes and at end

cut to—fast transition from one scene to another; indicates there is no time lapse

pan—movement of camera, either back and forth movement or following movement of a character

dolly in or back—camera moves toward or away from a person or object

long shot, medium shot or close shot—camera focuses from a distance; camera is closer, camera is very close

pov shot—(point of view shot) used to show what a person is looking at; camera focuses on what character looks at [4]

Camera Directions

Fade In

1. Heorot—night

    Shot 1   Camera pans over sleeping Geats in mead-hall lingering a little on Hondscio and longer on Beowulf. (Silence except for sleeping sounds)

    Shot 2   _____

                 _____

    Shot 3   _____

                 _____

    Shot 4   _____

                 _____

    Shot 5   _____

                 _____

    Shot 6   _____

                 _____

---

[4] Michelle Cousin, *Writing a Television Play* (Boston: The Writer, Inc., 1975) 9-12.

Name_____
Date_____

Shot 7 _____

_____

Shot 8 _____

_____

Shot 9 _____

_____

Shot 10 _____

_____

Shot 11 _____

_____

Shot 12 _____

_____

Shot 13 _____

_____

Shot 14 _____

_____

Shot 15 _____

_____

Shot 16 _____

_____

Shot 17 _____

_____

Shot 18 _____

_____

Lesson 4
Symbolism: The Necessary Monster

Objective
- To understand the monsters as symbols of dangers, fears, and evils which any society that seeks to survive must face

Notes to the Teacher
Although many of the characters and events in *Beowulf* can be documented by historical references, Beowulf and Grendel, the main characters, appear to be fictional. Beowulf is described as the strongest of men, but his swimming feats are all that make him seem unrealistic. Robinson argues that the impossibly long swims attributed to Beowulf could be the result of inaccurate translation,[1] making Beowulf a real and believable character. If Robinson is right, then Grendel, his mother and the dragon are the only nonrealistic characters. Perhaps Grendel symbolizes, as Tolkien argues, God's enemies, the forces of evil in the world.[2]

In the poem they are presented as real, in the sense that the Danes and the Geats believed in their existence on earth, but they also seem to represent the dangers and fears faced by the Anglo-Saxons in a sometimes hostile environment. In Anglo-Saxon life, feuds and warfare were a necessary defense against the plundering attacks of their cousins, the Vikings.

According to the Danes, Grendel's feud against Hrothgar springs up without rhyme or reason. They cannot find an explanation for his attacks or his refusal to pay *wergild* (the man-price allotted by law) for his killings. But by the time Grendel begins his raids, the Danish warriors have nothing to do. Hrothgar has subdued his enemies; his fame has spread far and wide; only drinking and boasting in the mead-hall are left to occupy the warriors. In his speech after the defeat of Grendel's mother, Hrothgar warns Beowulf about complacency and pride.

Beowulf, like Hrothgar, presides over a peaceful, successful kingdom when he is attacked by the dragon. He seizes the opportunity to reenact the glorious fights of his youth against the advice of his council and fights nobly to defeat the dragon but dies of his wounds. Perhaps the monsters may be interpreted as representing the implacable evil which all humans must face but which can be defeated because they inevitably resurface in a finite world. Only God can bring about their ultimate defeat.

Monsters abound in folklore, myth, Gothic works, science fiction, comics and horror movies. Their prevalence and popularity indicate a need of the human psyche to face and defeat these symbols of fear. The popularity of horror movies manifests the delighted response to the symbolic defeat of evil through the graphic destruction of a monster. Besides fictional monsters, people in all parts of the world report monster sightings, especially in inaccessible places.

Procedure
1. Distribute **Handout 11**. Divide students in groups to discuss the questions in Part A. Ask one member of the group to take notes. Ask one member of each group to summarize the group's opinions for the class. Assign Part B of the handout.

---

[1] Fred C. Robinson, "Elements of the marvellous in the characterization of Beowulf," *Old English Studies in Honour of John C. Pope*, ed. by Robert B. Burlin, and Edward B. Irving, Jr. (Toronto, Canada: University of Toronto Press, 1974), 121-127.
[2] J. R. R. Tolkien, "Beowulf: The Monsters and the Critics," *An Anthology of Beowulf Criticism*, ed. by Lewis E. Nicholson (Freeport, New York: Books For Libraries Press, 1963), 51.

28

Beowulf/Grendel
Lesson 4
Handout 11

Name_____
Date_____

Monster Madness

The Return of the Yeti

The 'Proof': A plaster cast shows a yeti footprint—all 20 inches of it.

Yes, yeti. Kin of Big Foot, these hairy, smelly aberrations are called Skunk Apes when lurking in Fort Myers, South Broward, the Everglades and Tavernier. The Sasquatch hulks in the woods of Washington. The Abominable Snowman tracks up Mount Everest. The Bardin Booger haunts Palatka. [1]

Part A. Discuss with your group the following questions.

1. Why do people love stories about monsters?

2. It seems obvious that the *Beowulf* poet's audience believed in the real existence of Grendel and the dragon. Do you believe in the existence of such monsters as Bigfoot, the Loch Ness Monster, the Abominable Snowman?

3. What were some of the real dangers and fears which the Anglo-Saxons had to face? Do you think that the Danes were as successful in defeating them as Beowulf was in defeating the monsters?

4. What dangers and fears do the people of today contend with? How successful have our heroes been in defeating them?

5. Do you think that the love of monster tales may help people symbolically to deal with the evil of the world in which they live?

Part B. Write a narrative in which a modern hero defeats a modern monster.

[1] Geoffrey Tomb, "The Return of the Yeti," *The Miami Herald*, 4 August 1970, 4B.

Lesson 5
Theme

Objective

- To identify themes: heroism; loyalty between warrior, lord, and thane; kingship; and the struggle to transcend the inevitability of death

Notes to the Teacher

Beowulf exemplifies the pagan Anglo-Saxon heroic ideal. He is courageous and generous and never retreats from a fight or a feud. He is more eager for fame and glory than for gold. When he wins gold, he gives it to his king or his followers. In each of his three fights he is the consummate Anglo-Saxon warrior.

The Anglo-Saxon warrior fought for the glory of his lord. If his lord was killed in battle, a warrior was disgraced if he did not avenge the death or die in the attempt.

In *Beowulf* the Anglo-Saxon idea of kingship is important. From Schild Schafing to Hrothgar to Beowulf, the qualities that the Anglo-Saxons considered important in their kings are evident. The king had to be a good warrior in order to gain fame to attract fighting thanes, whom he rewarded generously for their loyalty. From the defeated came the gold to be distributed to loyal thanes in the mead-hall. The relationship between thane and king was most important. In several Anglo-Saxon lyrics the speaker bemoans the loss of his lord and the subsequent exile and loneliness of the formerly happy thane.

Procedure

1. Distribute **Handout 12**. Ask students to fill out the chart as class or homework and to answer the questions. Discuss the completed handout in class.
   Suggested Responses:

   Beowulf's motive: (Grendel) glory and to help Danes; (mother) finish job; more glory; help Danes; gold; (dragon) revenge for destruction of his town; recall youthful heroics; help his people; gold; fame

   Opponent's motive: (Grendel) unknown; perhaps envy of songs in mead-hall; (mother) revenge for death of her son; (dragon) revenge for stealing a piece of his treasure

   Preparation for battle: (Grendel) removes weapons and armor; lies awake to observe opponent; psychologically prepares; (mother) wears armor and carries weapons: (dragon) makes special iron shield; wears armor and carries weapons

   Weapons: (Grendel) strength and faith; (mother) sword, armor, shield, dagger and faith; (dragon) special shield, sword, dagger

   Strategy: (Grendel) surprise; (mother) no special plan; (dragon) special shield

   Attitude toward battle: (Grendel) confident; (mother) confident; (dragon) afraid, but determined

   Physical state: (Grendel) young and in top form; strongest man; (mother) same; (dragon) old and tired

   Behavior of thanes: (Grendel) try to help; (mother) wait patiently; refuse to believe in defeat, but afraid to expect a win; (dragon) run away in fear, except Wiglaf, who fights heroically at Beowulf's side

   Outcomes: Kills Grendel; kills Grendel's mother; kills dragon with Wiglaf's help but dies of his wounds

   1. *Courage; strength; skill with weapons; does not retreat; wins or dies in attempt; follows a code; motivated by fame, revenge, especially blood feuds, helping others; gold; generosity with rewards*

   2. *Expected to repay lord with their lives for the gold he gives them; suffer exile and disgrace if they do not aid their lord; rewards of gold and fame for loyalty*

   3. *Reasons will vary.*

   4. *Answers will vary.*

2. Distribute **Handout 13**. Allow students to work in pairs to reread the following four sections of the poem, fill in the handout lists, and answer the question: (1) opening description of Scyld and Hrothgar; (2) Hrothgar's warning speech to Beowulf during the celebration in the mead-hall after the killing of Grendel's mother; (3). Beowulf's speech just after slaying the dragon and giving Wiglaf his armor and sword; (4) the last seven lines of the poem.

Suggested Responses:

Hrothgar—good warrior, has many followers, famous, generous with followers, wise

Perils of power—greed, pride, forgetfulness of the source of power, forgetfulness of death

Beowulf—protected his people from attack, did what he was supposed to do, protected what was his, did not instigate fights, betrayed no one, killed no kinsmen

Last lines—kindest, most gentle and mild, eager for fame

Summary: Anglo-Saxon kings were expected to be good warriors, have many followers, be generous with rewards, and be famous.

3. Distribute **Handout 14**. Ask students if they think that the qualities necessary for leadership have changed since Anglo-Saxon times? *(Answers will vary.)* Ask them to name qualities expected of leaders today. *(Answers will vary.)* List responses on the chalkboard. Ask them to complete the assignment of **Handout 14**.

4. Distribute **Handout 15.** Give students a choice to design or describe their memorials.

5. Distribute **Handout 16**. Give students time to answer the questions. Discuss their answers.

Suggested Responses:

1. *Both Scyld and Beowulf are famous warriors and kings, buried with riches and honor. Both have a golden banner. Scyld is an orphan, but of noble lineage; Beowulf is living at his uncle's court, and in the end has no family left except Wiglaf.*

2. *Both Hrothgar and Beowulf are old, famous kings who have long ruled peacefully before attacked; Hrothgar, a monster, Beowulf, a dragon. Hrothgar's kingdom is demoralized; Beowulf's kingdom is destroyed. After Hrothgar's death, his kingdom is torn by civil strife resulting from the conflicting claims of Hrothmund and Hrothgar's sons to the throne. After Beowulf's death, his people are left leaderless, expecting war and exile.*

3. *To the Anglo-Saxons, fame was a way of transcending the finality of death. Their pagan religion made them keenly aware of the vagaries of fate and the suddenness and capriciousness of the end of life, prosperity, and peace. Scyld's memory is*

kept alive by the song of the scop, and Beowulf wants his barrow to keep his memory alive in the eyes of sailors who would use it as a landmark.

4. *The story begins with the death of a famous king and goes on to tell of the rise to and the loss of power and the death of another famous king. Therefore, events in the story come full circle.*

Students should mention that death is inevitable for all, even the most famous of heroes, but that there appears to be a cyclical aspect to events. When one leader falls, another eventually rises and falls in his own turn. Fame may preserve a man's name as long as memory lasts, but to a pagan, death is final.

6. Distribute **Handout 17** or assign for homework.

And the Winner Is . . .

Battle	Grendel	Grendel's mother	Fire dragon
Beowulf's motive			
Opponent's Motive			
Preparation for battle			
Weapons			
Strategy			
Attitude toward battle			
Behavior of thanes			
Outcomes			

Name_____
Date_____

Answer the following questions:

1. What are the attributes of an Anglo-Saxon hero?

2. What is expected of the followers of an Anglo-Saxon lord?

3. Would the Anglo-Saxon brand of heroism be an anachronism in today's world? Explain.

4. If you said yes to #3, what do you think constitutes heroism today?

Name_____
Date_____

Noblesse Oblige

Directions: List Hrothgar's kingly virtues and the perils of power against which Hrothgar warns Beowulf. List Beowulf's kingly virtues from his speech to Wiglaf and from the last lines of the poem.

Hrothgar as King

_____

_____

_____

_____

_____

Perils of Power

_____

_____

_____

Beowulf as King

_____

_____

_____

_____

_____

_____

The Geat's Tribute to Beowulf

_____

_____

_____

_____

Summarize the virtues which the Anglo-Saxons thought to be important in their leaders?

[1] Ruth P.M. Lehmann, trans., *Beowulf* (Austin: University of Texas Press, 1988), frontpiece.
[2] Ibid., 80.

Beowulf/Grendel
Lesson 5
Handout 14

Name_____
Date_____

Beowulf for President!

Directions: What if Beowulf were running for president and you were his campaign manager? Design a slogan and an ad to be used in his campaign.

Name_____

Date_____

Here Lies

Directions: Kevin Crossley Holland in his book, *Green Blades Rising*, says the following about the Anglo-Saxon thane.

> The well-born Anglo-Saxon layman had an ambition he could put a name to. He wanted to win fame for courage, loyalty, and dignity in the teeth of implacable fate. An Old Norse proverb goes, 'One thing I know never dies nor changes, the reputation of a dead man.' Anglo-Saxons would have said the same. The final word of *Beowulf* is 'lofgeornost', most eager for fame. [1]

Beowulf gives detailed instructions for his funeral and the memorial to his fame. If you could realize your ambition in life, what memorial would you wish? Describe or design your memorial and the ceremonies and remembrances which you think would make a fitting testament to the realization of your life's ambition.

[1] Kevin Crossley Holland, *Green Blades Rising* (New York: The Seabury Press, 1975), 61.

And the Wheel Keeps on Turning

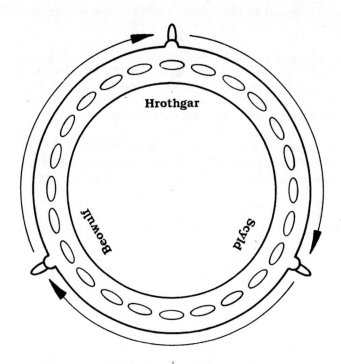

1. The opening of the poem is a description of Scyld's funeral while the ending is a description of Beowulf's funeral. What are the similarities which exist between Scyld and Beowulf?

2. What are the similarities between Hrothgar and Beowulf?

3. All three Anglo-Saxon leaders were eager for fame. Why was fame so important to the Anglo-Saxons?

4. In his warning speech to Beowulf, Hrothgar points out that death comes suddenly without warning. What conclusion can you draw about the theme of this work from the above?

Name_____
Date_____

Optional Writing Assignment

Write a comparison or contrast essay in which you compare Beowulf to a modern hero, real or fictional.

Lesson 6
Point of View

Objectives

- To recognize the effect of the author's choice of point of view on the reader
- To compare the effect of point of view on the reader in *Beowulf* and *Grendel*

Notes to the Teacher

Both *Beowulf* and *Grendel* use the first person point of view. In *Beowulf* the narrator is a scop who tells the story as he heard it, and he frequently intrudes into the story to forewarn and to comment on the action. Therefore, the effect of the narration is the same as the third person point of view, except that instead of the disembodied voice who describes the events, a flesh and blood "I" tells us about what he has heard. This technique combines the advantage of believability with the freedom to know and describe whatever the narrator wants to relate. *Grendel*, on the other hand, tells his own story. From chapter 1–12, the reader feels Grendel's feelings, thinks his thoughts, and receives impressions of his world through the senses and is caught up in the struggle to make sense of his experiences.

In *Beowulf*, Grendel's description is left to the listener's imagination and little motivation is provided for his actions. *Grendel* fills in these gaps. John Gardner gives us Grendel's description of himself as large and strong, hairy, with claws and teeth "like a saw." He can talk, reason, bleed, feel pain and emotion. At first he could be wounded by the sharp weapons of the Anglo-Saxons until the dragon puts a spell on him. He is a mammal, and he says once that he thinks that his mother has some human in her. The whole novel is a study of Grendel's struggle to find meaning for his existence and that of the men with whom he is so intimately and bloodily connected.

Gardner's use of Grendel's description also provides a counterpoint to the *Beowulf*-poet's admiring description of the Danes and Geats. The lesser of the heroic ideal which is only implied in *Beowulf* is shown clearly in *Grendel*. Instead of heroic perfection, Hrothgar and his people, struggle with a lifestyle that demands fighting and bloodshed and a religion which provides no answers. They do the best they can in a puzzling universe. Only Beowulf retains the heroic mystique, although he is depicted as cold-bloodedly insane.

Procedure

1. After students have read *Grendel*, review point of view. Ask the following questions:
    a. Who is telling the story? *(Grendel)*
    b. Do you feel sympathy with Grendel?
    c. If the story were told by a third person narrator, do you think you would have more or less sympathy with Grendel? Why?

2. Distribute **Handout 18**. Divide the class in half. Assign one-half to write an essay describing Grendel in the third person point of view, the other, in the first person point of view. When essays are finished, ask students to exchange essays with someone who wrote the other point of view and to read aloud to each other. Ask students to react to the different points of view. List their responses on the board.

3. Distribute **Handout 19**. In the first column is a description of the characters as the *Beowulf*-poet sees them. Assign students to work in small groups to describe each of the characters as Grendel sees them. Write descriptions on the blank lines. Ask students if they see any of the characters differently after having read *Grendel*.
    Suggested Response:
    Answers will vary. They should recognize that most of the characters are diminished, made more ordinary, human, especially Hrothgar and his men. Wealtheow seems more important and real than in Beowulf. The Shaper is made a real person, and his character is both exalted and diminished. Unferth's presence is explained; he achieves a kind of ironic yet sad heroism. Only Beowulf remains larger than life, but he is depicted as crazy.

    Suggested Responses: **Handout 19**
    Grendel's mother: She seems ineffective but caring. She wants to protect Grendel and to

41

to comfort him. She tries to nurse him. She apparently worries about him, and she is afraid of the world outside the cave. She is handicapped by her lack of language.

Hrothgar: He is a petty king with ambition. He doesn't seem to be able to do anything about Grendel although otherwise he makes some intelligent moves as a ruler. He does seem to have the loyalty of his people, but as he ages, he is weighed down by the burdens of kingship.

Wealtheow: She is young and beautiful and smart. Her function of preventing a feud between her people and Hrothgar's is clear. She accepts her position with grace rather than mere resignation.

The Shaper: He is the inspiration of the people. His blindness and the beauty and power of his songs are emphasized. Even Grendel cannot resist his poetry.

The Danes: They are ordinary soldiers, boastful, drunken, dreaming of being heroes, but mostly falling short.

Unferth: He is dreaming of heroism and willing to risk all, even death, but cruelly humiliated by Grendel's refusal to fight him fairly or kill him. He is living out his life in disgrace because suicide would be the cowardly way out and running away would be a cowardly lie.

Beowulf: He is cool, calculating, shrewd, very strong, treacherous and crazy.

4. Distribute **Handout 20.** Ask students to answer the questions after they have read the last chapter of Grendel.
Suggested Responses:
   1. anticipation, excitement, joy, fear desire for blood
   2. Beowulf pretends to be asleep but actually is observing Grendel's method and is ready when Grendel reaches for him. He uses surprise.
   3. Grendel says it is an accident.
   4. Beowulf is using psychological warfare. Grendel is demoralized by the technique. He imagines Beowulf as having wings and breath of fire.
   5. Grendel is amazed. He says it is an accident.
   6. Beowulf is seen as cool, calculating, clever and vicious. He uses surprise, strength and psychology to defeat Grendel. In the poem Beowulf's courage and strength are emphasized, not to mention his courtly

decision to fight Grendel bare-handed because weapons would not be fair. Grendel is shown as so fearful that he rips off his own arm in his desire to escape. In Gardner's story Beowulf's use of the element of surprise and the psychological tactics throw Grendel off balance enabling Beowulf to twist off Grendel's arm.

7. Yes, in Beowulf the hero is seen as courtly and chivalrous. He declares he will fight Grendel bare-handed because Grendel is not familiar with swordplay. Although he plans his strategy carefully and presses the advantage he gains by surprising Grendel, Beowulf is seen as a fair fighter who wins fair and square. In Grendel Beowulf appears slightly mad and somewhat cruel. He seems sneaky and calculating. His use of psychologically demoralizing whispers and his parody of the childish "Uncle [or] I give up" seem like taking unfair advantage. Also, he seems to use unnecessary violence. The courtliness has disappeared and in its place is a cruel, calculating, cold-blooded killing instinct.

8. Elements of grim humor include Grendel's remark that he would not want to wake up to the sound of his laugh any more than the Geats would; the napkin; the image of Grendel and Beowulf's shaking hands grotesquely.

5. Distribute **Handout 21.** Ask students to write a commentary on the fight between Beowulf and Grendel as if it were being reported by the announcer at a TV wrestling match.

The I's Have It!

Directions: Write a three-paragraph description of Grendel. Follow the plan given below:

Paragraph 1: background and habitat

Paragraph 2: physical description

Paragraph 3: mental, emotional, spiritual description

Write either in the *third person* point of view using only third person pronouns, such as he, she, it, they, them, or in the *first person* point of view using only first person pronouns, I, me, we, us, mine.

To write in third person, think of yourself as perched outside of what you are describing, but with a view that allows you to see everything, even to read Grendel's mind.

To write in first person, imagine that you are Grendel. Think his thoughts and feel his feelings. Look at the world through his eyes.

Name_____
Date_____

The Eyes of Grendel Are Upon Us

Beowulf-poet		Grendel
"monstrous hag, rabid and raging, resolved on revenge"	Grendel's mother	_____ _____ _____
old, wise, famous, a peer-less king, many followers, success in war	Hrothgar	_____ _____ _____
"high-born, gentle manners, gracious, wise of word"	Wealtheow	_____ _____ _____
sings a sweet song, a skillful poet, knows ancient stories	The Shaper	_____ _____ _____
"mighty host, lordly warriors, li[ving] in gladness, boldly boasted"	The Danish Warriors	_____ _____ _____
jealous of his warrior reputation, challenging Beowulf at first, later admitting Beowulf's heroism	Unferth	_____
strongest man alive, "fearless, gallant, great of heart," courteous	Beowulf	_____ _____ _____

Name_____
Date_____

Psychology vs. Strength

Directions: Answer the following questions:

1. What are Grendel's feelings as he approaches the mead-hall?

2. What trick allows Beowulf to gain the upper hand at the very first moment of the encounter with Grendel?

3. How does Grendel explain Beowulf's gaining the upper hand?

4. Why does Beowulf whisper to Grendel? What is the effect of his whispering on Grendel?

5. How does Grendel feel when he realizes that he is going to die? What is his explanation for his defeat?

Reread the fight scene between Beowulf and Grendel in *Beowulf*. Answer the following questions:

6. What details of the fight are explained or amplified in *Grendel*?

7. Does the account in *Grendel* change the traditional image of Beowulf? How?

8. Grim humor is present in this scene in *Grendel* but not in *Beowulf*. Give examples.

Name_____
Date_____

And in This Corner . . .

Directions: Imagine that you are the sports commentator at a wrestling match. Describe the fight between Beowulf and Grendel. Give the combatants appropriate names and don't forget to have the referee go over the rules before the match.

You might even want to interview the winner and the loser after the match is over.

Lesson 7
Structure

Objective
- To identify the structure of the story

Notes to the Teacher
The actual story in *Grendel* occurs in only five of the twelve chapters. The other seven chapters are flashbacks, establishing the character of Grendel, the Danish history, and the reasons for the feud between Grendel and Hrothgar. In chapter 1, Grendel and the Danes are introduced in the twelfth year of Grendel's feud with Hrothgar. Chapter 2 is a flashback in which Grendel reminisces about his youth and first encounter with men. In succeeding chapters the flashback gradually reveals the background to the revelations in chapter 1. Chapter 7 returns to a point midway through the twelfth year of the feud, but flashes back to the second year of Grendel's raiding. Chapter 9 returns Grendel to December of the twelfth year. Chapter 10 continues the story of the last year with the death of the Shaper. In chapter 11, Beowulf arrives, and in chapter 12, Grendel dies.

The technique of flashback is useful because if allows the older Grendel to look back in an effort to understand his motives. If an omniscient third person narrator were telling the story, it could proceed chronologically, but it would be more difficult to elicit sympathy for Grendel. Since the story is really Grendel's agonized attempt to make sense out of his own existence and to explain his murderous raids on Hrothgar's people, the first person point of view is highly appropriate. The story is almost a confession novel, except that Grendel refuses absolution, maintaining to the end that everything is accident; nothing matters.

Procedure
1. Distribute **Handout 22**. Ask students to fill in the section of the outer box labeled Chapter 1, Exposition, with the time of year, place, characters, and number of years that Grendel's war has been going on. Ask students to summarize the events of chapters 2–8 in the inner box labeled Chapters 2–8, Flashback, and for the last 4 chapters in the section of the outer box labeled Chapters 9–12.

Suggested Responses:

Outer box: Chapter 1, Exposition

It is spring, the beginning of the twelfth year of Grendel's war; a mountainous, forested country; a town with a mead-hall atop a hill. The speaker is Grendel; other characters; his mother, Hrothgar, the king, the old Shaper, and Hrothgar's people. Grendel has been at war with them for twelve years.

Inner box: Chapters 2–8, Flashback

Grendel tells about his childhood in the cave, his first time out of the cave, and the accident when the bull attacked him and his first encounter with men. Grendel spies on Hrothgar's town and describes his wars and the growth of his power. Grendel sees the arrival of the Shaper and the building of Hrothgar's great mead-hall. The Shaper's poetry inspires Grendel to try to join the men, but they are afraid and attack him. Grendel goes to the dragon. The dragon puts a spell on him. Grendel begins his feud with Hrothgar's men. Grendel encounters Unferth and humiliates him. (In chapter 7 the time briefly returns to midway through the last year of Grendel's feud, but then flashes back to Hrothgar's marriage to Wealtheow. Grendel almost kills her. Hrothulf arrives.)

Outer box: Chapters 9–12

It is December of the twelfth year of Grendel's war. Grendel is filled with strange fears; encounters the old priest; kills a mountain goat. The Shaper gets sick and dies. Beowulf arrives. Beowulf is welcomed by Hrothgar. Grendel fights Beowulf and dies as a result of the fight.

Grendel's motivation is so convincing because it is revealed as the agonized musings of an adult creature looking back for some meaning and reason to his life. If the story had begun with young Grendel, the point of view would have had to change. It would have been more difficult to arouse the reader's sympathy for Grendel.

47

Name_____
Date_____

Composition

Chapter 1   **Chapters 9–12**

Chapters 2–8

Flashback

Exposition   Rising Action,
                                                                      Turning Point,
                                                                      Denouement

Lesson 8
Character Development

Objectives

- To trace Grendel's development from a fascinated spectator of men's activities to a cold-blooded killer of men
- To explore reasons behind Grendel's feuding
- To identify heroism in the characters
- To identify traits of the anti-hero in Grendel and Unferth

Notes to the Teacher

Grendel could be classified as a psychological or even a confessional novel since much of the novel is an interior monologue in which Grendel, the main character, searches for a meaning to his existence. The other characters play a subordinate role as measures against which Grendel hopes to find definition. He observes, discusses, terrifies and sometimes eats them in an attempt to discover if he matters or not.

Although Grendel is a monster, he shares intelligence, language, and a search for meaning with the humans who inhabit his world. He is fascinated by humans, especially their poetry and music. He cannot reconcile the reality of bloodshed, drunken boasting and betrayal with the idealistic heroism expressed by the singing in the mead-hall. He refuses to recognize the nobility, sacrifice, or heroism in Hrothgar, Wealtheow, or Unferth. He sees only cunning machinations, futile waste of beauty, and silly posturing in their attitudes.

In most of the novel, he agonizes over why he keeps killing the Danes and whether he should stop or not. He finds no answers to his questions nor does he get comfort from his mother or his shadowy ancestors; the dragon's explanations are either incomprehensible or unsatisfyingly close to his own pessimistic vision. He scornfully rejects the inspiration provided by the Shaper's beautiful songs that clothe the deeds of Hrothgar's people in heroic nobility whether deserved or not.

Grendel could be viewed as a psychological study. What causes Grendel to become a maneater? Is it an unhappy childhood? Is it rejection? Grendel himself calls it a sickness. Or is it the charm turned curse because now that weapons are useless, nothing can stop his marauding?

Grendel has characteristics of an anti-hero. He calls himself the world-rim walker, outcast and outlawed. He rejects Danish society, politics, ideals, and religion. He tries and fails to find a better answer than accidental meaninglessness. He tries and fails to be accepted by men.

Yet the reader cannot hate him for even in his evilness, he evokes sympathy and sorrow while he gobbles down Hrothgar's thanes. Will he somehow be saved by his love for the Shaper's singing? Will he reject the wisdom of the dragon? It does not happen. He falls to his death whispering his litany: the world has no meaning; everything is *accident*.

Procedure

1. Distribute **Handout 23**. Allow students to work in small groups to find the references and to answer the questions in chapters 2–6. After discussing their findings, ask whether any one incident stands out as the main reason for Grendel's feud.

Suggested Responses:

Chapter 2—*Grendel is trapped in a tree. The men, at first, think he is a tree fungus: then they decide he is a spirit that eats pigs. The king, in fear, attacks him with an ax; he is saved by the appearance of his mother. He says they are dangerous because they think and scheme, and he calls them crazy.*

Chapter 3—*Grendel is emotionally affected by the Shaper's songs, but he calls the words lies. He feels torn apart because the reality of what he observes does not match the fine beauty and idealism of the Shaper's words.*

Chapter 4—*Grendel decides to convert after he hears the Shaper singing about the creation of the world and how he is the dark side of creation. He goes toward the mead-hall calling for mercy and peace, but the Danes attacked him with their weapons. He wishes for someone to talk to. He returns because he says he is addicted. He wants the Shaper's songs to be true even if he has to be the outcast.*

Chapter 5—*The dragon says that Grendel inspires the Danes and improves them, that if there were no Grendel, they would invent another to take his place because they need a monster. Therefore, Grendel, himself, is irrelevant. It will make no difference whether he stops or not; nothing will change.*

Chapter 6—*Grendel at first feels that the charm has defeated his enemies. He then realizes that now he has nothing to fear and nothing to stop him; his raids become a kind of inevitability. He discovers the charm when he accidentally runs into a guard, trips and is not hurt by the guard's sword. He has discovered a reason for his existence and is now the "Ruiner of Mead-halls, Wrecker of Kings."*

Opinions will vary as to the main reason for the feud.

2. Distribute **Handout 24**. Ask students to imagine that Grendel is explaining to Hrothgar why he began the feud, and why he is entitled to consideration despite his murders. Tell them to model their speech that Frankenstein's monster makes to Dr. Frankenstein. Allow students who are good at dramatic interpretation to perform their speeches for the class.

3. Distribute **Handout 25**. Ask students what being a hero means to them. List their responses on the chalkboard. Formulate a consensus description of a hero. As a class, work on the descriptions of the three characters. Ask students to write their paragraphs individually as homework. When they have finished, ask for volunteers to read their answers aloud.
Suggested Responses:

Hrothgar's heroism is the patient kind which does not give up even when he realizes that Grendel cannot be stopped with Danish weapons, that his treaty with the Helmings will probably be broken, that Hrothulf will very likely try to take his kingdom from his sons.

Unferth does not hide, run away or commit suicide in spite of the fact that he has been cheated out of his heroic clash with Grendel by Grendel's refusal to fight him. He tries to make himself hope for Beowulf's success.

Wealtheow carries out her duties as Hrothgar's Queen with grace in spite of Grendel's raids and her brother's hatred of Hrothgar. She

soothes Unferth and treats Hrothulf with kindness in spite of his danger to her sons. Beowulf's heroism is self-confident and sure, unafraid of danger. His eyes stare unfocused. He seems coolly insane to Grendel. The Danes are afraid of his lashing tongue.

4. Distribute **Handout 26**. Explain that the anti-hero is common in modern fiction. This type of hero can be defined as the opposite of the traditional hero. Some examples of anti-heroes are Cervantes's *Don Quixote*, Heathcliff in Emily Bronte's *Wuthering Heights*, Leopold Bloom in James Joyce's *Ulysses*, and Yossarian in Joseph Heller's *Catch 22*. Ask students to follow the directions on **Handout 26** to identify Grendel and Unferth as anti-heroes.
Suggested Responses:
Grendel: (1) It is because he murders and the Danes cannot punish him; (2) He sneaks around the town and mead-hall at night, spying, and when he tries to join them, they attack him; (3) He makes fun of the Danes and rejects all they stand for; (4) He keeps searching for answers but can only come up with meaninglessness; (5) He is crude, but the other descriptions don't fit. He isn't stupid or dishonest. Whether he is a failure can be argued. He is successful in his feud with the Danes, at least for twelve years, but he is a failure at establishing any answers or happiness for himself; (6) He often says he is angry.

Unferth: (1–3) They don't fit because although he did kill his brother, he made restitution according to society's law; (4) Some will argue that he tries for even greater heroism than the other Danes when he chases Grendel, and that he is forced to achieve an ideal which the other Danes might not understand because of the way Grendel humiliates him; (5) He seems to be a failure as a hero, yet he achieves an even more difficult kind of heroism by not giving up even in the face of humiliation, and he was involved in a crude and stupid mistake in his past; (6) Yes, he is angry.

Name_____
Date_____.

Profile of a Killer

Directions: Grendel does not begin his systematic killing of the Danes, his war as he calls it, all at once. Use the references below to trace the steps which led up to his declaring the blood feud.

Chapter 2:   Describe Grendel's first encounter with men. Why does he call them "the most dangerous things I'd ever met"? What does he conclude about them?

Chapter 3:   What is Grendel's first reaction to the Shaper's songs? Why does he describe himself as "torn apart by poetry"?

Chapter 4:   Describe Grendel's conversion. How do the Danes react to him? What does he wish for? Why does he go back again two nights later?

Chapter 5:   What is the dragon's answer to Grendel's question of why he should not stop scaring the Danes?

Chapter 6:   Why does Grendel say that he thought the dragon's charm an advantage *at first*? How does Grendel discover the charm? What is Grendel's explanation of the "strange, unearthly joy" that he feels after beginning his raids? What other result becomes apparent to him?

Name_____
Date_____

The Monster Talks Back

Directions: Another famous monster has no name, but he is known to everyone by the name of his creator, Frankenstein. Frankenstein's monster gives the following explanation to his creator for his murder of Frankenstein's brother. If Grendel were to give a similar speech to Hrothgar explaining his murders of Hrothgar's thanes, what would he say? Write the speech as Grendel would say it.

How can I move thee? Will no entreaties cause thee to turn a favourable eye upon thy creature, who implores thy goodness and compassion? Believe me, Frankenstein: I was benevolent; my soul glowed with love and humanity: but am I not alone, miserably alone? You, my creator, abhor me; what hope can I gather from your fellow-creatures, who owe me nothing? they spurn and hate me. The desert mountains and dreary glaciers are my refuge. I have wandered here many days; the caves of ice, which I only do not fear, are a dwelling to me, and the only one which man does not grudge. These bleak skies I hail, for they are kinder to me than your fellow-beings. If the multitude of mankind knew of my existence, they would do as you do, and arm themselves for my destruction. Shall I not then hate them who abhor me? I will keep no terms with my enemies. I am miserable, and they shall share my wretchedness. Yet it is in your power to recompense me, and deliver them from an evil which it only remains for you to make so great that not only you and your family, but thousands of others, shall be swallowed up in the whirlwinds of its rage. Let your compassion be moved, and do not disdain me. Listen to my tale: when you have heard that, abandon or commiserate me, as you shall judge that I deserve. But hear me. The guilty are allowed, by human laws, bloody as they are, to speak in their own defence before thy are condemned. Listen to me, Frankenstein. You accuse me of murder; and yet you would, with a satisfied conscience, destroy your own creature. Oh, praise the eternal justice of man! Yet I ask you not to spare me: listen to me; and then, if you can, and if you will, destroy the work of your hands. [1]

[1] Mary Shelley, *Frankenstein* (New York: Dutton, 1912), 101-102.

Beowulf/Grendel
Lesson 8
Handout 25

To Be or Not To Be . . . a Hero

Directions: Although Grendel refuses to recognize it, the Danes and the Geats do manage to achieve a measure of heroism in spite of their faults. On the lines next to each name, describe the heroism of each of the following characters:

Hrothgar _____
_____
_____

Unferth _____
_____
_____

Wealtheow _____
_____
_____

Beowulf _____
_____
_____

Which comes closest to your idea of heroism? Answer in a paragraph or two.

Beowulf/Grendel
Lesson 8
Handout 26

Name_____
Date_____

The Anti-hero

Directions: Both Grendel and Unferth exhibit characteristics of the anti-hero, who frequently appears in modern literature, the opposite of the traditional hero. Examine the list of anti-hero traits. Not all anti-heroes will possess all of these traits. List the number of the trait and an example or explanation of why you chose it under the name *Grendel* and under the name *Unferth*. A trait may apply to only one or to both.

Traits of the Anti-hero

1. Deprived of the rules and consequences of society

2. Outlaw; has no status in society; must wander on fringes of society

3. Rejects values, rules, attitudes of society and political establishment

4. Seeks to establish his own rules and ethics

5. A failure, crude, sometimes stupid or even dishonest

6. Often angry

Grendel

_____

_____

_____

_____

_____

Unferth

_____

_____

_____

_____

_____

Lesson 9
Humor and Symbolism

Objectives

- To define black humor and identify examples in *Grendel*
- To recognize the importance of the number 12 in the novel structure

Notes to the Teacher

John Gardner is noted for his facility with different genres and languages and for his eclectic style. Several critics have commented on his poetic prose. In *Grendel* Gardner mixes poetry, myth, allusion and black humor in Grendel's interior monologue. He evokes the heroic language of *Beowulf* with poetry, kennings, and sentences reminiscent of the rhythm and phrasing of lines of Anglo-Saxon poetry. He sustains the tone of despairing nihilism through images, such as "the cold mechanics of the stars" and the mood of dark foreboding with images of spiders around the moon and vines turning to snakes in his hand. The dragon becomes a symbol of evil. Throughout the novel Grendel's grim resignation to meaninglessness and absurdity is underscored by his sardonic, cynical, bitter, disillusioned, morbid humor, a type of humor often called black humor because its material is derived from the dark side of life.

Since there are so many elements of style in *Grendel*, this lesson concentrates on humor, one aspect with which students may identify. The author's use of the number 12 will arouse curiosity.

In *Grendel*, Gardner uses the number 12 as a unifying device and a symbol of continuity. Grendel raids for twelve years; the novel has 12 chapters; each chapter corresponds to a sign of the zodiac, the path of the sun in its daily and yearly march across the sky. Although Grendel's musings jump back and forth in time, the steady march of the chapters, following the twelve signs of the zodiac, forms a progression which holds the story together and represents continuity as well as the 12 years of Grendel's feud.

Procedure

1. Explain that Grendel often uses humor. Ask them to read in chapter 12 the example of his use of the tablecloth as a napkin. Ask: Why could this type of humor be termed *black humor*. Ask them to give examples of this type of humor which they have encountered elsewhere.
   Suggested Responses:
   It is morbid and disgusting to use a napkin to catch blood when you eat somebody.

2. For homework, assign them to search through the novel to find more examples of humor. Alert them that they will use the examples in the next assignment.

3. Distribute **Handout 27**. Divide the class into 4 teams. Give them a limited time to list as many examples of black humor from *Grendel* as they can. Use a format such as: G. uses napkin, p. 168. Suggest that they divide chapters of the book among the team members. When time is called, ask one member of each team to collect papers from the team; make a neatly copied list eliminating duplicate examples. Post the lists; reward the winning team.

4. Distribute **Handout 28**. Explain that ancient astronomers divided the path of the sun across the sky into twelve signs. They named each sign after the constellation which the sun crossed in its apparent movement. Divide the class into teams of two or three. Ask them to look for the sign in each chapter and copy the line and page number of the reference.
   Suggested Responses:
   1. *Example provided.*
   2. *"Then some thirty feet away, there was a bull." (p. 19)*
   3. *"It was late spring. Every sheep and goat had its wobbly twins." (p. 44)*
   4. *"The sun backs away from the world like a crab and the days grow shorter, the nights grow longer, more dark and dangerous." (p. 46)*
   5. *"No use of a growl, a whoop, a roar, in the presence of that beast!" (p. 57)*
   6. *"The shaper talked . . . how here and here alone in all the world men were free and heroes were brave and virgins were virgins." (p. 77)*
   7. *"Balance is everything, riding out time . . ." (p. 91)*

8. *"And so—I watch in glee—they take in Hrothulf; quiet as the moon, sweet scorpion." (p. 113)*

9. *"The trees are an arrow in a dead man's chest." (p. 125)*

10. *"I watch a great horned goat ascend the rocks toward my mere." (p. 139)*

11. *"I kiss the ice on the frozen creeks, I press my ear to it, honoring the water that rattles below, for by water they come: . . ." (p. 151)*

12. *" . . . but where the water was rigid there will be fish, and men will survive on their flesh 'til spring." (p. 170)* [1]

[1]John Gardner, *Grendel* (New York: Vintage Books, A Division of Random House, Inc., 1989), 5–170, *passim.*

Name_____

Date_____

Black Humor

Directions: List as many examples of humor as you can find in the time allotted.

Example: G. apologizes and tips his imaginary hat to the oak trees, p. 7

_____

_____

_____

_____

_____

_____

_____

_____

_____

_____

_____

_____

_____

_____

_____

_____

_____

_____

_____

_____

_____

_____

_____

_____

_____

_____

_____

_____

Name_____
Date_____

Astrology Anyone?

Directions: Each chapter in *Grendel* corresponds to one of the signs of the zodiac, beginning with chapter 1, the ram. In each chapter, find the reference to the sign. Copy the sentence and page number.

Chapter 1   Aries the Ram

"The old ram stands looking down over rockslides, stupidly triumphant." (p. 5)

Chapter 2   Taurus the Bull

_____
_____

Chapter 3   Gemini the Twins

_____
_____

Chapter 4   Cancer the Crab

_____
_____

Chapter 5   Leo the Lion

_____
_____

Chapter 6   Virgo the Virgin

_____
_____

Chapter 7   Libra the Balance

_____
_____

Chapter 8   Scorpio the Scorpion

_____
_____

Chapter 9   Sagittarius the Archer

_____
_____

Chapter 10 Capricorn the Goat

_____
_____

Chapter 11 Aquarius the Water Bearer

_____
_____

Chapter 12 Pisces the Fishes

_____
_____

Lesson 10
Theme

Objectives
- To identify the theme of nihilism expressed by Grendel
- To examine and question the nihilistic attitudes of Grendel and the dragon against the optimistic outlooks of Unferth and Beowulf

Notes to the Teacher
The pessimism expressed by Grendel from his opening description of the sun spinning mindlessly in the sky to his closing assertion that all is accident seems overwhelming, yet it is, in conclusion, not convincing. He deliberately chooses a mindless, meaningless interpretation of every event. In spite of all of his ironic revelations of the hypocrisy of Hrothgar's Danes, his railing against the seeming lies of the Shaper's vision which clothes their petty feuds in glorious, heroic illusion, he does not succeed in desecrating the essential nobility of man's aspirations. Though man's efforts may not match his ideals, meaning derives from the recognition of the higher goal and the attempt to achieve it. Failure is the refusal to strive. As Unferth says, it is recognizing the "values beyond what's possible [that makes] the . . . struggle . . . worthwhile." Grendel is, after all, defeated by a man, a pattern-maker, who asserts meaning and defeats the nihilistic monster with words. Grendel is beaten not by weapons or strength but by Beowulf's cool, planned strategy and his whispers that promise renewal.

The dragon, whom one critic called Grendel's God and who symbolizes evil, tells Grendel that since man needs a monster to define himself and to provide inspiration for improvement, Grendel might as well be the one. "If you withdraw, you'll instantly be replaced," the dragon tells him. Thus, Grendel finally accepts the evil vision of the dragon and begins his raids, but not until the dragon stacks the deck by providing a charm making it impossible for the Danes to wound Grendel. In one sense, Grendel has sold his soul to the devil. Eventually he loses his life but is not redeemed. He falls into blackness with a curse on all life, "Poor Grendel's had an accident, *so may you all.*"

Students need to recognize that the author makes Grendel choose the nihilistic outlook but that the novel ultimately refutes the choice. The search for a meaning to man's existence in a universe that seems chaotic is a common theme in Gardner's works and in the work of many authors in many centuries.

Procedure
1. Distribute **Handout 29**. If students have studied *Macbeth* recall the play. If not explain that Macbeth became king of Scotland after murdering the rightful king. He had been the hero who helped the king win a civil war. After he becomes king, Macbeth is so obsessed with protecting his throne and passing it on to his descendants that he engages in a series of bloodier and ever more senseless murders while seeking the counsel of the weird sisters (witches) who mislead him with half-truths. The soliloquy is spoken as Macbeth prepares to fight a rebel army. He has just received news of his wife's suicide, and he is beginning to recognize that the witches have misled him. He is killed by one of his thanes, Macduff, who crosses the sea from England where he has gone to join the rebel army.

2. Before beginning the assignment, ask students what they think the phrase *nihil ex nihilo* means. Read the soliloquy aloud. Answer the questions on the handout. Discuss the responses.
   Suggested Responses:
   1. *Grendel says "tedium is the worst pain.";
   that the sun walks overhead. He describes the waiting for the Shaper to die. The chapter is filled with references to the past and to a dark future. Time passes slowly and boringly.*
   2. *Grendel pictures the Danes as fooled by the Shaper's lies and as fooling themselves about the reality of their actions. He sees Unferth as a fool for clinging to his heroic ideals. In chapter 1, he describes his feud with Hrothgar as "an idiotic war" and himself as a "pointless, ridiculous monster."*

61

3. Grendel often describes himself as a shadow (chapter 10) and as walking around the edges of the world or the outside of the mead-hall at dusk. In chapter 1, he plays the mind game of standing outside himself and looking at himself as he is posturing. He repeats this device frequently. Hrothulf's arrival and the encounter with the priest Ork (chapter 9) are written like a play with scenes and dialogue.

4. Yes, Grendel would agree. He says repeatedly that he is stupid and life is meaningless. He describes himself as constantly whispering. He cannot communicate with the Danes because his language is older than theirs although similar. Also, his voice is too loud and frightful for them to decipher the sounds. His killings, an expression of his anger, and, ironically, the meaning that he derives from the story he tells is summarized in his phrase at the close of chapter 10, "Nihil ex nihilo."

3. Distribute **Handout 30**. Allow ample time for preparation. Assign two debate teams of two students each to debate the *for* and the *against* sides of the proposition. In addition, assign a timekeeper and two students to act as scorekeepers to collect, add and display the scores. If students are eager to participate, several pairs of teams can be assigned. If there are several debates, students might discuss what factors contributed to the different scores and winning sides.

4. Distribute **Handout 31** which may be used as an alternate to **Handout 30** or as a culminating activity. Allow ample time for preparation. Ask students to conduct a murder trial of Grendel. Appoint a judge, a team of prosecutors and defense lawyers, court reporter, an officer to swear in witnesses, and someone to be Grendel, the defendant. The remainder of the class will act as jury and witnesses. The prosecutor and defense lawyer may engage their own witnesses from the class. In addition to Grendel's mother, Hrothgar, Unferth, the dragon, etc., they may wish to bring in expert witnesses, such as a psychologist or zoologist. Allow the jury time to deliberate apart from the class. Reconvene the court to announce the verdict.

Name_____
Date_____

Nothing from Nothing

Directions: Grendel's theme is that there is no meaning to existence. A famous character, unlike Grendel a noble man, who became a monster as he engaged in a series of bloody murders, expresses the same philosophy. Like Grendel he chose not to learn from experience; he gives in to despair. He makes clear his attitude in a famous soliloquy, spoken just before he is killed by the leader of a rebel army, a defeat which he deluded himself into believing could never happen because he had been told by witches that he lived a charmed life. The character is Macbeth, the tragic anti-hero of Shakespeare's *Macbeth*.

Read Macbeth's soliloquy, and answer the questions below.

Macbeth Act V. Scene V

> Tomorrow, and tomorrow, and tomorrow
> Creeps in this petty pace from day to day
> To the last syllable of recorded time;
> And all our yesterdays have lighted fools
> The way to dusty death. Out, out, brief candle!
> Life's but a walking shadow, a poor player,
> That struts and frets his hour upon the stage
> And then is heard no more. It is a tale
> Told by an idiot, full of sound and fury,
> Signifying nothing. [1]

1. In the first lines Macbeth personifies time as creeping slowly. Compare Grendel's comments about time in chapter 10.

2. To Macbeth people are fools heading for the grave. Would Grendel agree with Macbeth's description? Explain.

3. In lines 6, 7 and 8 Macbeth pictures man as an insubstantial actor showing off on the stage of life and forgotten after death. In what way is Grendel "a walking shadow [and] a poor player/That struts and frets his hour upon the stage"? What about the Danes?

4. Macbeth says that life "is a tale/Told by an idiot, full of sound and fury,/Signifying nothing." Would Grendel agree? Explain.

[1] William Shakespeare, *Macbeth*, New York: Washington Square Press, 1959), 86.

Name_____

Date_____

Nothing or Something

Directions: Two teams will debate the merits of Grendel's viewpoint. The rest of the class will act as judges and rate the winning team.

Resolved: Since the world and everything in it is unplanned accident, existence is meaningless; the past is irrelevant; nothing matters.

For: This team will take the attitude that the proposition is true. They will try to prove it by using the arguments and experiences of Grendel and of the dragon.

Against: This team will take the attitude that the proposition is false. They will try to prove it by using the arguments of Unferth, Beowulf, the Shaper, Ork, and any other evidence in the story.

Rules:

1. No evidence is admissible unless it can be supported by the novel.

2. Each team will have three, two-minute chances to speak. In the first two minute period they will present their argument. The second two minute period will be used for rebuttal. In the rebuttal period, a team may argue only points which the other side has presented. The third two-minute period will be a summation.

3. At the close of debate, the rating will be collected, added, and results published.

Debate Score Sheet

Rating chart:

Rate the arguments on a scale of 1 to 3.

> 3 = most arguments very persuasive

> 2 = most arguments moderately persuasive or arguments about equally divided between persuasive and non-persuasive

> 1 = most arguments not very persuasive

	For	Against
period 1 presentation	_____	_____
period 2 rebuttal	_____	_____
period 3 summation	_____	_____

Name_____

Date_____

Monster on Trial

Directions: Participate in a trial of Grendel, either as judge, member of jury, court officer, court reporter, prosecutor, defense lawyer, the defendant, or a witness.

> Judge: presides over the trial, makes rulings on questions of procedure, instructs jury

> Court Officer: swears in witnesses; announces verdict

> Court Reporter: keeps record of proceedings

> Jury: makes the determination of guilt or innocence based on the evidence

> Prosecutor: plans the prosecution of Grendel; selects witnesses and conducts the trial; makes summation for prosecution at end of the trial

> Defense Lawyer: plans the defense of Grendel; selects witnesses and conducts the defense; makes the summation for the defense at the end of the trial

> Witnesses: take the stand and testify either for the prosecution or defense; may be either friendly or hostile

Name_____

Date_____

Crossword Puzzle

Across Clues

1. King of the Geats
2. Beowulf and Wiglaf's family name
6. Hrothgar's famous mead-hall
7. The first Danish King
10. Hero who defeats Grendel
11. Beowulf's sword
13. Had swimming contest with Beowulf
17. King of the Danes
18. Hrothgar's people
19. The sword that Unferth lent to Beowulf to fight Grendel's mother
21. Anglo-Saxon poet, historian, singer
22. Location of the Geats

Down Clues

1. The Queen of the Geats
3. Hrothgar's favorite thane; eaten by Grendel's mother
4. Monster who raided Heorot for twelve years
5. Translation: hall of the _____
8. Hrothgar's spokesman who taunts Beowulf about Breca
9. Fought side by side with Beowulf against the dragon
12. The Queen of the Danes
14. Ancestor of Grendel
15. Nephew of Hrothgar who later betrays him
16. Beowulf killed him but died in the fight
18. Location of the Danish tribe
20. Beowulf's people

Name_____

Date_____

Test
Beowulf: Part A

Part 1: Matching

_____ 1. He lends his sword to Beowulf

_____ 2. Grendel's mother kills him

_____ 3. King of the Danes

_____ 4. The only thane who helps Beowulf fight the dragon

_____ 5. The name of Hrothgar's famous mead-hall

_____ 6. Anglo-Saxon poet

_____ 7. Beowulf had a swimming match with him

_____ 8. The name of Beowulf's tribe

_____ 9. Monster who attacked Hrothgar's hall for twelve years

_____ 10. Beowulf's sword

a. Aeschere	h. Hrunting
b. Breca	i. Hygelac
c. Danes	j. Naegling
d. Geats	k. Scyld
e. Grendel	l. Scop
f. Heorot	m. Unferth
g. Hrothgar	n. Wiglaf

Part 2: Multiple Choice

_____ 11. The setting of *Beowulf* is in
   a. England
   b. Denmark
   c. Sweden
   d. Denmark and Sweden
   e. the moors and the fens

_____ 12. *Beowulf* was probably written about the year
   a. 441
   b. 597
   c. 725
   d. 1066
   e. 1492

_____ 13. All but one of the following statements about the author of *Beowulf* are true. Choose the one that is false.
   a. He is a Christian.
   b. He is unknown.
   c. He is either Danish or Swedish.
   d. He knows the Bible and Latin literature.
   e. He knows Anglo-Saxon history and culture.

_____ 14. A clever descriptive comparison, such as whale-road for the sea, is called a
        a. alliteration
        b. *caesura*
        c. kenning
        d. scan
        e. scop

_____ 15. In this line, "Lo, we have listened to many a lay," which letters are alliterated?
        a. a
        b. h
        c. l
        d. m
        e. t

_____ 16. In this line, "Of the Spear-Danes' fame, their splendor of old," the pause comes between which two words?
        a. the//Spear-Danes
        b. Spear-Danes//fame
        c. fame//their
        d. their//splendor
        e. splendor//of

_____ 17. The process of marking the stressed and unstressed syllables in a line of poetry is known as
        a. alliterating
        b. kenning
        c. rhyming
        d. rhymical
        e. scanning

_____ 18. In all Beowulf faced and killed ___ adversaries.
        a. 1
        b. 2
        c. 3
        d. 4
        e. 5

_____ 19. Which of his adversaries did Beowulf face without weapons?
        a. the dragon
        b. Grendel
        c. Grendel's mother
        d. all of these
        e. none of these

_____ 20. Beowulf died of the wounds he received as a result of the fight with
        a. Breca
        b. the dragon
        c. Grendel
        d. Grendel's mother
        e. Unferth

Name_____

Date_____

_____ 21. Hrothgar warned Beowulf against the dangers of
     a. death
     b. dragons
     c. monsters
     d. pride and greed
     e. war

_____ 22. Which statement about Beowulf's thanes is true?
     a. They were always loyal.
     b. They fought at his side in every fight.
     c. They gave up and left with Hrothgar's men in the fight with Grendel's mother.
     d. They ran away from the dragon.

_____ 23. The language of *Beowulf* is
     a. English
     b. Danish
     c. Old English
     d. Swedish
     e. unknown

_____ 24. Probably the most important thing to the Anglo-Saxon hero was
     a. fame
     b. gold
     c. becoming king
     d. service
     e. winning

_____ 25. Anglo-Saxon poetry contains ___ strong beats in each line.
     a. 0
     b. 1
     c. 2
     d. 3
     e. 4

Name_____

Date_____.___

Test
Grendel: Part B

Directions: Study the following statements. Write *G* if the statement is true only for *Grendel*. Write *B* if the statement is true only for *Beowulf*. Write *E* if the statement is true for both works.

_____ 26. Grendel's motive is unknown.

_____ 27. Grendel has a charm which protects him from weapons.

_____ 28. The dragon placed the charm on Grendel.

_____ 29. Beowulf is cool, calculating and crazy.

_____ 30. A dragon appears in the story.

_____ 31. The story is told from Grendel's point of view.

_____ 32. The Danes and Geats appear as noble and heroic.

_____ 33. Beowulf psychologically tortures Grendel by whispering in his ear as they fight.

_____ 34. Grendel is hairy and can speak.

_____ 35. Unferth tries to fight Grendel, but Grendel refuses to fight him.

Suggested Essay Topics

Compare or contrast:

1. Beowulf's three fights

2. the tone of *Grendel* with the tone of *Beowulf*

3. the Unferth of *Beowulf* with the Unferth of *Grendel*

4. the Hrothgar of *Beowulf* with the Hrothgar of *Grendel*

Other approaches:

5. Describe a contemporary monster, such as drugs or nuclear warfare. Tell how long its victims have been in danger of attack, what the monster does to them, and how the victims are affected by the attacks.

6. Pretend you are Grendel's psychiatrist. Write a case history in which you explain his illness and its causes.

7. Using the information from both *Beowulf* and *Grendel*, describe the position of women in Anglo-Saxon society.

8. Critics believe that the *Beowulf*-poet was a Christian telling a story set in pagan times to Christian listeners. In *Beowulf* there are references both to fate (Wyrd) and to the Christian God. Trace the references to both pagan and Christian gods and explore the reasons why you think the poet may have used both in his poem.*

*Some critics have said that the Christian references were added later by a Christian recorder of a pagan poem, but this idea is no longer fully accepted.

Answer Key: Crossword Puzzle

Answer Key: Test, Part A

1. m	11. d	21. d
2. a	12. c	22. d
3. g	13. b	23. c
4. n	14. c	24. a
5. f	15. c	25. e
6. l	16. c	
7. b	17. e	
8. d	18. c	
9. e	19. b	
10. j	20. b	

Answer Key: Test, Part B

26. B

27. E

28. G

29. G

30. E

31. G

32. B

33. G

34. G

35. G

Bibliography

Beowulf

Abrams, M. H., Ed. *The Norton Anthology of English Literature.* New York: W. W. Norton & Company, 1979.

Blair, Peter Hunter. *An Introduction to Anglo-Saxon England.* 2nd ed. Cambridge, England: Cambridge University Press, 1977.

Bloom, Harold, Ed. *Beowulf, Modern Critical Interpretations.* New York: Chelsea House Publishers, 1987.

Brooke, Stopford A. *The History of Early English Literature.* Freeport, New York: Books for Libraries Press, 1982.

Burlin, Robert B. and Irving, Edward B., Jr., Eds. *Old English Studies in Honour of John C. Pope.* Toronto, Canada: University of Toronto Press, 1974.

Cohen, Robert and Harrop, John. *Creative Play Direction.* Englewood Cliffs, New Jersey: Prentice-Hall, Inc., 1974.

Costello, Mary Enda; Goll, Paulette S.; Jacobs, Stephen L.; Maloney, Eileen K. *Shakespearean Comedies.* Rocky River, Ohio: The Center for Learning, 1984.

Cousin, Michelle. *Writing a Television Play.* Boston: The Writer, Inc., 1975.

Crossley-Holland, Kevin. *Green Blades Rising, The Anglo-Saxons.* New York: The Seabury Press, 1975.

Dobbie, Elliot Van Kirk, Ed. *Beowulf and Judith.* New York: Columbia University Press, 1953.

Goodridge, Janet. *Creative Drama and Improvised Movement for Children.* Boston: Plays, Inc., 1971.

Kennedy, Charles W. *Beowulf, The Oldest English Epic.* Charles W. Kennedy, Trans. Oxford, London, New York: Oxford University Press, 1968.

Lehmann, Ruth P. M. *Bewoulf.* Ruth P. M. Lehmann, Trans. Austin: University of Texas Press, 1988.

McDonnell, Helen; Pfordresher, John; Veidemanis, Gladys V. *England in Literature.* Glenview, Illinois: Scott Foresman and Company, 1985.

Nicholson, Lewis E., Ed. *An Anthology of Beowulf Criticism.* Freeport, New York: Books for Libraries Press, 1963.

Raffel, Burton. *Beowulf.* Burton Raffel, Trans. Robert P. Creed, Aftwd. New York: NAL Penguin Inc., 1963.

Stevens, Martin and Mandel, Jerome, Eds. *Old English Literature.* Lincoln, Nebraska: University of Nebraska Press, 1968.

Tomb, Geoffrey. "The Return of the Yeti." *The Miami Herald.* August 4, 1970.

Grendel

Ackland, Michael. "Blakean Sources in John Gardner's *Grendel*" in *Critique*. XXXIII: 57-65. No. 1, 1981. (found in "John Gardner" in *Twentieth Century American Literature*. III:1546-1565. Ed. by Harold Bloom. New York, New Haven, Philadelphia: Chelsea House Publishers, 1986.)

Bloom, Harold, Ed. "John Gardner" in *Twentieth Century American Literature*. III:1546-1565. New York, New Haven, Philadelphia: Chelsea House Publishers, 1986.

Cuddon, J. A. *A Dictionary of Literary Terms*. New York: Doubleday & Company, 1977.

Fugate, Francis L. *Viewpoint: Key to Fiction Writing*. Boston: The Writer, Inc., 1968.

Gardner, John. *Grendel*. New York: Vintage Books, A Division of Random House, Inc., 1971.

Holman, C. Hugh and Harmon, William. *A Handbook to Literature*. New York: Macmillan Publishing Company, 1986.

Knott, William C. *The Craft of Fiction*. Reston, Virginia: Reston Publishing Company, Inc., 1977.

May, Charles E. "Short Fiction: Terms and Techniques" in *Critical Survey of Short Fiction*. I:32-67. Ed. by Frank N. MaGill. Englewood Cliffs, New Jersey: Salem Press, 1981.

Nyren, Dorothy; Kramer, Maurice; Kramer, Elain Fialka, Eds. "John Gardner" in *Modern American Literature*. Vol IV, supplement to 4th Edition. pp. 181-187. New York: Continuum, 1989.

Riley, Carolyn and Harte, Barbara, Eds. "John Gardner" in *Contemporary Literature Criticism*. Vols. 2, 5, 8, 10, 18, 28, 34. Detroit, Michigan: Gale Research Company, 1974.

Shakespeare, William. *Macbeth*. New York: Washington Square Press, 1959.

Shelley, Mary. *Frankenstein*. Dutton, New York: Everyman's Library, 1965.

Acknowledgments

For permission to reprint all works in this volume by each of the following authors, grateful acknowledgment is made to the holders of copyright, publishers, or representatives named below.

Teacher Notes
Excerpt from *Twentieth Century American Literature, III*, Harold Bloom, ed., 1986. Published by Chelsea House Publishers, New York, New York.

Lessons 1, 2; Handouts 4, 7
Excerpts from *Beowulf, An Imitative Translation*, Ruth P.M. Lehmann, trans., 1988. Published by University of Texas Press, Austin, Texas.

Lessons 2, 3; Handouts 5, 6, 7, 8
Excerpts from *Beowulf, The Oldest English Epic* by Charles W. Kennedy, trans., 1940. Published by Oxford University Press, New York, New York.

Lesson 2, Handout 7
Excerpt from *Beowulf*, Howell D. Chickering, Jr., trans., 1977. Published by Doubleday & Co., New York, New York.

Lesson 2, Handout 7
Excerpts from *Beowulf*, translated by Burton Raffel. Copyright © 1962 by Burton Raffel. Reprinted by permission of the publisher, New American Library, a division of Penguin Books USA Inc.

Novel/Drama Series

Novel

Absolutely Normal Chaos/
Chasing Redbird, Creech

Across Five Aprils, Hunt

Adam of the Road, Gray/
Catherine, Called Birdy, Cushman

The Adventures of Huckleberry Finn,
Twain

The Adventures of Tom Sawyer, Twain

Alice's Adventures in Wonderland/
Through the Looking-Glass, Carroll

All Creatures Great and Small, Herriot

All Quiet on the Western Front, Remarque

All the King's Men, Warren

Animal Farm, Orwell/
The Book of the Dun Cow, Wangerin, Jr.

Anna Karenina, Tolstoy

Anne Frank: The Diary of a Young Girl,
Frank

Anne of Green Gables, Montgomery

April Morning, Fast

The Assistant/The Fixer, Malamud

The Autobiography of Miss Jane Pittman,
Gaines

The Awakening, Chopin/
Madame Bovary, Flaubert

Babbitt, Lewis

The Bean Trees/Pigs in Heaven,
Kingsolver

Beowulf/Grendel, Gardner

Billy Budd/Moby Dick, Melville

Black Boy, Wright

Bless Me, Ultima, Anaya

Brave New World, Huxley

The Bridge of San Luis Rey, Wilder

The Brothers Karamazov, Dostoevsky

The Call of the Wild/White Fang, London

The Canterbury Tales, Chaucer

The Catcher in the Rye, Salinger

The Cay/Timothy of the Cay, Taylor

Charlotte's Web, White/
The Secret Garden, Burnett

The Chosen, Potok

The Christmas Box, Evans/
A Christmas Carol, Dickens

Chronicles of Narnia, Lewis

Cold Mountain, Frazier

Cold Sassy Tree, Burns

The Color of Water: A Black Man's Tribute
to His White Mother, McBride

The Count of Monte Cristo, Dumas

Crime and Punishment, Dostoevsky

Cry, the Beloved Country, Paton

Dandelion Wine, Bradbury

Darkness at Noon, Koestler

David Copperfield, Dickens

Davita's Harp, Potok

A Day No Pigs Would Die, Peck

Death Comes for the Archbishop, Cather

December Stillness, Hahn/
Izzy, Willy-Nilly, Voigt

The Divine Comedy, Dante

The Dollmaker, Arnow

Don Quixote, Cervantes

Dr. Zhivago, Pasternak

Dubliners, Joyce

East of Eden, Steinbeck

The Egypt Game, Snyder/
The Bronze Bow, Speare

Ellen Foster/A Virtuous Woman, Gibbons

Emma, Austen

Fahrenheit 451, Bradbury

A Farewell to Arms, Hemingway

Farewell to Manzanar, Houston &
Houston/*Black Like Me*, Griffin

Frankenstein, Shelley

From the Mixed-up Files of Mrs. Basil E.
Frankweiler, Konigsburg/
The Westing Game, Raskin

A Gathering of Flowers, Thomas, ed.

The Ghost Walker/The Dream Stalker,
Coel

The Giver, Lowry

The Good Earth, Buck

The Grapes of Wrath, Steinbeck

Great Expectations, Dickens

The Great Gatsby, Fitzgerald

Gulliver's Travels, Swift

Hard Times, Dickens

Hatchet, Paulsen/
Robinson Crusoe, Defoe

Having Our Say, Delany, Delany, and
Hearth/*A Gathering of Old Men*, Gaines

The Heart Is a Lonely Hunter, McCullers

Heart of Darkness, Conrad

Hiroshima, Hersey/*On the Beach*, Shute

The Hobbit, Tolkien

Homecoming/Dicey's Song, Voigt

The Hound of the Baskervilles, Doyle

The Human Comedy/
My Name Is Aram, Saroyan

Incident at Hawk's Hill, Eckert/
Where the Red Fern Grows, Rawls

Invisible Man, Ellison

Jane Eyre, Brontë

Johnny Tremain, Forbes

Journey of the Sparrows, Buss and Cubias/
The Honorable Prison, de Jenkins

The Joy Luck Club, Tan

Jubal Sackett/The Walking Drum,
L'Amour

Julie of the Wolves, George/
Island of the Blue Dolphins, O'Dell

The Jungle, Sinclair

The Killer Angels, Shaara

Le Morte D'Arthur, Malory

The Learning Tree, Parks

Les Miserables, Hugo

The Light in the Forest/
A Country of Strangers, Richter

Little House in the Big Woods/
Little House on the Prairie, Wilder

Little Women, Alcott

Lord of the Flies, Golding

The Lord of the Rings, Tolkien

The Martian Chronicles, Bradbury

Missing May, Rylant/
The Summer of the Swans, Byars

Mrs. Mike, Freedman/
I Heard the Owl Call My Name, Craven

Murder on the Orient Express/
And Then There Were None, Christie

My Antonia, Cather

The Natural, Malamud/
Shoeless Joe, Kinsella

Nectar in a Sieve, Markandaya/
The Woman Warrior, Kingston

Night, Wiesel

A Night to Remember, Lord/*Streams to*
the River, River to the Sea, O'Dell

1984, Orwell

Number the Stars, Lowry/
Friedrich, Richter

Obasan, Kogawa

The Odyssey, Homer

The Old Man and the Sea, Hemingway/
Ethan Frome, Wharton

The Once and Future King, White

O Pioneers!, Cather/
The Country of the Pointed Firs, Jewett

Ordinary People, Guest/
The Tin Can Tree, Tyler

The Outsiders, Hinton/
Durango Street, Bonham

The Pearl/Of Mice and Men, Steinbeck

The Picture of Dorian Gray, Wilde/
  Dr. Jekyll and Mr. Hyde, Stevenson

The Pigman/The Pigman's Legacy, Zindel

The Poisonwood Bible, Kingsolver

A Portrait of the Artist as a Young Man,
  Joyce

The Power and the Glory, Greene

A Prayer for Owen Meany, Irving

Pride and Prejudice, Austen

The Prince, Machiavelli/*Utopia*, More

The Prince and the Pauper, Twain

Profiles in Courage, Kennedy

Pudd'nhead Wilson, Twain

Rebecca, du Maurier

The Red Badge of Courage, Crane

Red Sky at Morning, Bradford

The Return of the Native, Hardy

A River Runs Through It, Maclean

*Roll of Thunder, Hear My Cry/
  Let the Circle Be Unbroken*, Taylor

Saint Maybe, Tyler

Sarum, Rutherfurd

The Scarlet Letter, Hawthorne

The Scarlet Pimpernel, Orczy

A Separate Peace, Knowles

*Shabanu: Daughter of the Wind/
  Haveli*, Staples

Shane, Schaefer/
  The Ox-Bow Incident, Van Tilburg Clark

Siddhartha, Hesse

*The Sign of the Chrysanthemum/
  The Master Puppeteer*, Paterson

*The Signet Classic Book of Southern Short
  Stories*, Abbott and Koppelman, eds.

Silas Marner, Eliot/
  The Elephant Man, Sparks

The Slave Dancer, Fox/
  I, Juan de Pareja, De Treviño

Snow Falling on Cedars, Guterson

Something Wicked This Way Comes,
  Bradbury

Song of Solomon, Morrison

The Sound and the Fury, Faulkner

Spoon River Anthology, Masters

*A Stranger Is Watching/
  I'll Be Seeing You*, Higgins Clark

The Stranger/The Plague, Camus

Summer of My German Soldier, Greene/
  Waiting for the Rain, Gordon

A Tale of Two Cities, Dickens

Talking God/A Thief of Time, Hillerman

Tara Road/The Return Journey, Binchy

Tess of the D'Urbervilles, Hardy

Their Eyes Were Watching God, Hurston

*Things Fall Apart/
  No Longer at Ease*, Achebe

To Kill a Mockingbird, Lee

To the Lighthouse, Woolf

Travels with Charley, Steinbeck

Treasure Island, Stevenson

A Tree Grows in Brooklyn, Smith

Tuck Everlasting, Babbitt/
  Bridge to Terabithia, Paterson

The Turn of the Screw/Daisy Miller, James

Uncle Tom's Cabin, Stowe

The Unvanquished, Faulkner

Walden, Thoreau/*A Different
  Drummer*, Kelley

Walk Two Moons, Creech

Walkabout, Marshall

Watership Down, Adams

The Watsons Go to Birmingham—1963,
  Curtis/*The View from Saturday*,
  Konigsburg

When the Legends Die, Borland

Where the Lilies Bloom, Cleaver/
  No Promises in the Wind, Hunt

Winesburg, Ohio, Anderson

The Witch of Blackbird Pond, Speare/
  My Brother Sam Is Dead, Collier and
  Collier

A Wrinkle in Time, L'Engle/*The Lion, the
  Witch and the Wardrobe*, Lewis

Wuthering Heights, Brontë

The Yearling, Rawlings/
  The Red Pony, Steinbeck

Year of Impossible Goodbyes, Choi/*So Far
  from the Bamboo Grove*, Watkins

Zlata's Diary, Filipovic'/
  The Lottery Rose, Hunt

Drama

Antigone, Sophocles

Arms and the Man/Saint Joan, Shaw

The Crucible, Miller

Cyrano de Bergerac, Rostand

Death of a Salesman, Miller

A Doll's House/Hedda Gabler, Ibsen

The Glass Menagerie, Williams

The Importance of Being Earnest, Wilde

Inherit the Wind, Lawrence and Lee

Long Day's Journey into Night, O'Neill

A Man for All Seasons, Bolt

Medea, Euripides/
  The Lion in Winter, Goldman

The Miracle Worker, Gibson

Murder in the Cathedral, Eliot/*Galileo*,
  Brecht

The Night Thoreau Spent in Jail,
  Lawrence and Lee

Oedipus the King, Sophocles

Our Town, Wilder

*The Playboy of the Western World/
  Riders to the Sea*, Synge

Pygmalion, Shaw

A Raisin in the Sun, Hansberry

1776, Stone and Edwards

She Stoops to Conquer, Goldsmith/
  The Matchmaker, Wilder

A Streetcar Named Desire, Williams

Tartuffe, Molière

*Three Comedies of American Family Life:
  I Remember Mama*, van Druten/
  Life with Father, Lindsay and Crouse/
  You Can't Take It with You, Hart and
  Kaufman

Waiting for Godot, Beckett/*Rosencrantz
  & Guildenstern Are Dead*, Stoppard

Shakespeare

As You Like It

Hamlet

Henry IV, Part I

Henry V

Julius Caesar

King Lear

Macbeth

The Merchant of Venice

A Midsummer Night's Dream

Much Ado about Nothing

Othello

Richard III

Romeo and Juliet

The Taming of the Shrew

The Tempest

Twelfth Night

The Center for Learning

To Order Contact: **The Center for Learning—Shipping/Business Office**
P.O. Box 910 • Villa Maria, PA 16155
800-767-9090 • 724-964-8083 • Fax 888-767-8080

The Publisher

All instructional materials identified by the TAP® (Teachers/ Authors/Publishers) trademark are developed by a national network of teachers whose collective educational experience distinguishes the publishing objective of The Center for Learning, a nonprofit educational corporation founded in 1970.

Concentrating on values-related disciplines, the Center publishes humanities and religion curriculum units for use in public and private schools and other educational settings. Approximately 500 language arts, social studies, novel/drama, life issues, and faith publications are available.

While acutely aware of the challenges and uncertain solutions to growing educational problems, the Center is committed to quality curriculum development and to the expansion of learning opportunities for all students. Publications are regularly evaluated and updated to meet the changing and diverse needs of teachers and students. Teachers may offer suggestions for development of new publications or revisions of existing titles by contacting

The Center for Learning

Administrative/Editorial Office
21590 Center Ridge Rd.
Rocky River, OH 44116
(440) 331-1404 • FAX (440) 331-5414
E-mail: cfl@stratos.net
Web: http://www.centerforlearning.org

For a free catalog containing order and price information and a descriptive listing of titles, contact

The Center for Learning

Shipping/Business Office
P.O. Box 910
Villa Maria, PA 16155
(724) 964-8083 • (800) 767-9090
FAX (888) 767-8080